"Where is he?" Torin called, his voice raw with pain.

Zendric glanced behind him. But before a word could leave his lips, a winged demon swooped down from behind the Town Hall.

The creature looked like a gigantic cousin to the quasit, fat and bloated, its gray-green skin the color of a rotting corpse. With one swift motion, it plucked Zendric off the terrace and hauled him high over Main Square.

"Useless people of Curston"—Lexos laughed as he strode up the steps toward the Town Hall—"who will save you now?"

HAWTHORNE

REVELATIONS

PART 1:
PROPHECY OF THE DRAGONS

PART 2:
THE DRAGONS REVEALED
(August 2006)

∎ ∎ ∎ ∎ ∎

PROPHECY
OF THE DRAGONS

REVELATIONS, PART I

MATT FORBECK

COVER & INTERIOR ART
EMILY FIEGENSCHUH

MIRROR
STONE

HAWTHORNE

PROPHECY OF THE DRAGONS
REVELATIONS, PART 1
©2006 Wizards of the Coast, Inc.

Cover and interior art by Emily Fiegenschuh
Cartography by Rob Lazzaretti

First Printing: June 2006
Library of Congress Catalog Card Number: 2005935553

9 8 7 6 5 4 3 2 1

ISBN-10: 0-7869-4031-X
ISBN-13: 978-0-7869-4031-8
620-95559740-001-EN

U.S., CANADA,
ASIA, PACIFIC, & LATIN AMERICA
Wizards of the Coast, Inc.
P.O. Box 707
Renton, WA 98057-0707
+1-800-324-6496

EUROPEAN HEADQUARTERS
Hasbro UK Ltd
Caswell Way
Newport, Gwent NP9 0YH
GREAT BRITAIN
Please keep this address for your records

Visit our web site at www.mirrorstonebooks.com

For Savannah and Delaney

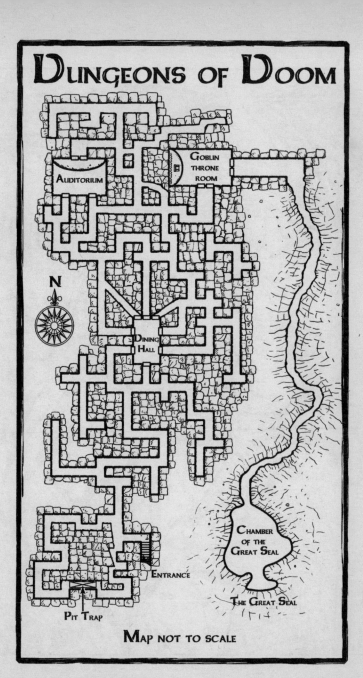

Dungeons of Doom

Auditorium

Goblin Throne Room

N

Dining Hall

Entrance

Pit Trap

Chamber of the Great Seal

The Great Seal

Map not to scale

CHAPTER

1

K nights of the Silver Dragon?" the demon snarled. "What's so dragonlike about you?"

Driskoll stared up at the thing floating above him. Its glowing red eyes bulged under the small, black horns on its head. It bared its teeth, knifelike bits of white that would have been more at home in the mouth of a shark than this warty, green-skinned creature.

"We're knights, not dragons," Moyra said to the demon. Although she only had a year on Driskoll, she always seemed stronger and more confident than he could imagine. Perhaps it had to do with the fact that she still had both of her parents, even if one of them—her father—was the most notorious thief in town.

A pair of halflings at the far end of the alley flinched as the demon flew toward them for a moment then back toward Driskoll, his brother, Kellach, and their friend Moyra.

"Don't anger it!" the male halfling said through trembling lips, as he threw his arm around his female companion.

"You're the ones who screamed for help," Driskoll said, unable to keep the irritation from his voice.

"You're just lucky we happened to be walking by," Kellach said, stroking the metal skin of Lochinvar, his clockwork dragonet. Locky perched on Kellach's shoulder like a pirate's parrot.

Driskoll didn't feel so lucky himself as he stared at his older brother. What in the Abyss had Kellach been thinking, leading them into this blind alley? Saving people was one thing. As Knights of the Silver Dragon it was their duty to help preserve Curston. Getting killed in the process, though, didn't seem so smart.

"Are you scared yet?" the fluttering demon asked with a hungry grin.

Driskoll realized he was sweating, and he heard what he could only describe as the fires of eternal damnation crackling from behind the creature, getting closer every second. He glanced at Kellach and Moyra for help, but they both stood gaping at the tiny beast, their eyes wide with terror.

The demon spun about three times, then reached toward them with its long, thin claws. As it did, it spat a single word:

"Boo."

Something in Driskoll's head burst open, and he sprinted screaming from the alley. As he raced toward the light spilling in from the street at the alley's mouth, he heard Kellach and Moyra's feet pounding behind him, along with the flapping of Lochinvar's foil-thin wings. Moyra tried to elbow Driskoll aside and take the lead, but Driskoll would have nothing of it. He shoved back at her and pumped his legs even faster.

Just as Driskoll's face cleared the end of the alley, he hurtled headlong into someone—or something. He and Moyra went down in a tangle of arms at the newcomer's feet.

A hand reached down and pulled Driskoll up into the air by the back of his collar, and he screamed, "It's got me! Help!"

"Shush, boy!" a stern voice said.

Driskoll spun around, trying to wrench himself free, and found himself nose to nose with an aged elf with steely blue eyes and long, white hair held back with a silver clasp.

"Zendric!" Driskoll couldn't remember the last time he'd been so happy to see the old wizard.

"Sharp as ever, I see," Zendric said, setting Driskoll on his feet. Moyra and Kellach scrambled to stand next to the wizard.

"What seems to be the hurry?" Zendric brushed off his charcoal-colored robes.

A pair of screams came down the alley, the same sound that had brought Kellach, Moyra, and Driskoll into the shadows in the first place.

"Ah," the wizard nodded, looking at Kellach. "What is it?"

"A quasit demon," Kellach said.

Locky hissed, "Bad beast-y."

"And how can you be so sure it was a quasit?" Zendric arched a silvery eyebrow at the boy.

Kellach frowned. "It matches the description and illustration in *A Practical Guide to Monsters*. If you'd—"

Zendric cut the boy off with a wave of his hand. "Well done," he said, a faint smile curling his lips. "I don't recall permitting you to thumb through my books, however."

Kellach flushed, then stood aside as Zendric strode toward the mouth of the alley. Before he entered it, he turned back to the three kids.

"Demons such as these have the power to inspire fear in the hearts of those who gaze upon them, no matter how foolish they may appear." He looked into each of their eyes in turn. "The terror you feel now is an enchantment, not something in your hearts. It will pass soon. For now, remain here."

With that, the wizard turned and marched into the alley.

Driskoll watched as Zendric disappeared into the gloom. Then he nudged Kellach in the arm.

"Don't you think we should lend him a hand?

Kellach snorted, "Do you think he needs it?"

"If Zendric can't handle that thing," Moyra said, "then what chance would we—?"

An earsplitting scream echoed from the far end of the alley. A loud bang followed.

Then Driskoll heard a tinny, two-voiced cheer. A moment later, the overjoyed halflings came scurrying out of the alley's mouth, with Zendric shooing them from behind.

"Yes, yes, yes," the wizard said. "I shall take you up on your kind offer for dinner at a later date. At the moment, though, I'm afraid I'm in a bit of a rush. My apologies, of course. Best wishes to you and your kin."

"No thanks for us?" Moyra asked the halflings.

"For what?" the female said with a scowl. "Nearly getting us killed? Next time, I'll thank you to—"

Moyra stomped toward the halfling. The halfling grabbed her companion's tiny hand and pulled him away at top speed.

As the halflings dashed north up Cutthroat Court, Zendric turned to Kellach, Driskoll, and Moyra and frowned. "Let's go," he said, heading south without waiting to see if they would follow.

Kellach fell into step right beside Zendric, trying to match his stride. Driskoll and Moyra scrambled to catch up.

Zendric's head snapped back and forth as he scanned the streets. Kellach mimicked him. Driskoll noted they were heading toward Main Square, the heart of the city. When he and the other kids walked through Broken Town—this oldest and most abused part of Curston—they kept their wits about them. Cutpurses and killers strolled the streets here freely, often looking for prey. Zendric and Kellach, though, seemed to be ready for something more.

"What's a demon doing wandering around in Curston?" Moyra asked.

"Demons are not uncommon in this town," Zendric said. "When the place bore the name of Promise, such things were unheard of, but I'm afraid we now live in a different, darker place."

"We expect to see demons during the night," Driskoll said. "That's why Dad has the whole town under a curfew from dusk till dawn. But during the day?"

"Your father keeps Curston under curfew because he's the captain of the watch," Zendric said. "If things continue as they have, he may be forced to change from a simple curfew to full-day martial law."

Driskoll stumbled but managed to catch himself. "What?" he asked. "Why?"

"Quasits are natural cowards. When minor demons become so bold, their more powerful brethren cannot be far behind."

Zendric glanced over his shoulder as he made a final turn and headed into Main Square. Driskoll, Kellach, and Moyra plunged after him into the stands and shops that sprawled across the open plaza.

"What are you saying?" Moyra asked.

"The Seal—which was only partly repaired after the Sundering five years ago—is breaking down again. Soon, it will fall apart completely, and the most powerful demons of the Abyss will lay siege to Curston once more."

Driskoll stopped and stared at the wizard's back. "Can't we do something to stop it?"

Zendric looked over his shoulder and smiled. "That, boy, is why I gathered you to me. Now step lively."

Driskoll scrambled to catch up.

Zendric veered away from the vendors in Main Square and started up the marble steps of one of the largest, most majestic buildings in Curston, the Town Hall. A towering block of cut white stone, it stood at the east end of the square, staring over the market at the Cathedral of St. Cuthbert across from it. The wide, long stairs led up thirty steps to an open terrace of polished granite lined with tapered columns.

"So what's our plan?" Kellach asked.

The wizard turned to look back at Kellach, Driskoll, and Moyra as they followed him up the stairs.

"Haven't you been listening, boy?" he asked. "Why do you think I've brought you here, to this great hall? Why do you think I've gathered together you three, the newest members of our reconstituted Knights of the Silver Dragon? Our plan to save Curston will be determined in conference with the most powerful figures in our fair town. Right here. Right now."

CHAPTER

2

As Driskoll, Kellach, and Moyra swept into the building's foyer behind Zendric, the wizard pointed past the painted busts of the greatest leaders in the city's history and toward the chamber's right. There, marble stairs wound along the bright yellow walls to the gallery above.

Driskoll stared up at the old elf. "You mean you want us to sit all the way up there?"

Zendric sighed. "I believe you deserve to be in the main room as much as anyone. However, not everyone feels the way I do, and since we're in a hurry it seems more prudent to simply have you observe. Afterward, I will attempt to answer any questions you might have."

"These people think we should be treated like children," Kellach said, unable to mask his irritation.

"I never said that." Driskoll's father, Torin, strolled into the foyer from the large, dim room beyond.

Torin nodded a greeting at his sons and Moyra, then gave Zendric a short bow. His uniform looked as if he'd slept in it, perhaps sitting up. The bags under his eyes seemed darker than usual, and the hair at his temples had started to show gray through the brown.

Driskoll couldn't remember seeing his father ever look so worn. Thinking back, he realized he hadn't seen his father in days, although that wasn't unusual. As captain of the watch, Torin's duties kept him busy. He often came home after his sons were fast asleep and sometimes left before they were up—or slept until long after they were gone for the day.

Now, though, he looked like he'd been on his feet for the better part of a week. His eyes were bloodshot, and worry furrowed his brow. When he spoke again, Driskoll scarcely heard him.

"It's not a matter of what you deserve," Torin said in a hoarse voice. "It's about what's safest for you."

"I'm fourteen, and I can handle anything in this building," Kellach said. As he spoke, Locky cringed, curling around the back of his master's neck.

"We're not kids," Driskoll said.

"You're my kids," Torin said. "That means you'll listen to me. Now get upstairs before I have Gwinton toss you out on your rears."

Driskoll peered past his father to see the dwarf in watcher's garb wave a greeting at them. Then Gwinton jerked his salt-

and-pepper beard at Torin. "They're waiting for you, sir." He looked up at Zendric. "And for you too."

Moyra grabbed the boys' hands and led them away upstairs as the adults strode into the main chamber.

"It's not fair," Driskoll said.

"It's not a matter of being fair," Moyra said. "If we want to know what's happening here, we need to play along—for now."

"Dad didn't look happy," Kellach said.

"Does he ever?" asked Moyra, as they emerged into the empty upper gallery. They moved down the stairs that cut through the few rows of seats until they reached the stone railing overlooking the vast chamber below. A domed ceiling stretched above them. It had been painted to resemble a sunny sky filled with puffy clouds, but Driskoll almost couldn't make this out in the shadows. Indirect light spilled in from the ring of wide-open windows that ran along the top edge of the walls, but it seemed to fade in strength before illuminating much at the level of the floor.

A wide, long table stood upon a raised dais and stretched across the far end of the hall. A handful of the most powerful people in Curston sat behind the table, glowering at one another and at the people still trickling into the hall to fill the seats.

Driskoll recognized his father and Zendric, who sat next to each other near the center of the table. Next to them sat Pralthamus, the town's magistrate, and the other members of the city's ruling council—two men and a woman. Driskoll had heard his father grumble about them after work sometimes, but he'd only met them once or twice.

"Look, here comes Latislav," Moyra said.

Driskoll spied the head cleric of St. Cuthbert's in his sky blue robes, leaning on his gnarled staff as he made his way to an empty chair next to Zendric.

"I never liked him much," Driskoll said.

"He's better than Lexos," Kellach said, referring to the cleric Latislav had replaced months ago. Also the city's former magistrate, Lexos had wielded tremendous power in Curston, power he'd lost when the three Knights had exposed his role in an attempt on Zendric's life.

Moyra shuddered. "I'm glad he got trapped in that cave in the mountains," she said. "I hope we never see him again."

"I'll take Latislav any day," Kellach said. "You just don't like going to church, Driskoll."

"How would I know? We haven't been but a handful of times since Mom disappeared."

Moyra gasped, "But Jourdain hasn't been seen since the Sundering of the Seal. Are you saying you haven't been to church in five years? Even Breddo takes me more often than that."

"Only because he's looking for the heaviest purses to slit," Driskoll said.

"What are you saying?" Moyra said, glaring at Driskoll.

"Hush," Kellach said, stepping between the others. "They're about to start."

11

Zendric stood up and cleared his throat. Through some enchantment, it sounded to Driskoll as if the wizard were standing right next to him. Everyone else fell silent.

"Thank you, my fellow citizens of Curston, for coming to our mutual aid at this, our darkest hour since the Sundering of the Seal. As many of you know, the frequency and severity of the attacks on our town have grown in recent weeks." At this, Zendric looked down at Torin, who gave him and the crowd a grim nod. The wizard continued.

"These and other signs can only mean that we have come finally to the third verse of the Prophecy of the Dragons recorded so many years ago, just after the founding of our fair home."

"What of the Seal?" a portly man in the front row said, standing so that all could hear his words. "I thought you'd repaired it."

Zendric frowned. "After the Seal was sundered five years ago, I and the few remaining members of the Knights of the Silver Dragon endeavored to remake it. As our continuing problems with monsters of all sorts should indicate, we only partly succeeded."

The wizard leaned forward, putting his hands on the table before him. "I have consulted with those friends of ours who made the ultimate sacrifice to help us. They contacted me at their own great peril. They tell me that our time is short.

"As it stands now, the Seal is like the piece of broken cork stuffed back into the end of a cask. It leaks, dripping evil around its edges. Soon enough, these broken bits will fail entirely, and the evil of the Abyss will come gushing out once more."

A gnome stood upon her chair, trembling so much that Driskoll could see it even from the upper gallery. "And what do you propose to do about it?"

Zendric nodded as if the woman had posed to him the most incredible riddle he'd ever heard. Then he sighed. "We must prepare for war."

A murmur ran through the crowd.

"All is not lost," Zendric said. "Despite our failures in the past, I have made preparations to employ the Key of Order to re-create the Seal anew. This is a desperate plan, to be sure, but these are desperate times in which we live."

"How can you know that this will work?" Latislav said.

The wizard looked down at the cleric with a bemused smile. "I don't," he said. "If I did, I would have attempted it long ago. But it seems now there are no other options for us."

"When will you depart?" Torin said, his face like a rock. "How long do we have?"

"I will leave immediately. With a bit of luck on our side, and perhaps the favor of the gods—who have little love for the creatures of the Abyss—we may prevail."

A man stood up in the back of the chamber. Looking down, Driskoll recognized him as Durmok, the adventurer whom he, Kellach, and Moyra had discovered the first time they'd ventured into the Dungeons of Doom. He looked less sure of himself now than he had then, even when he'd been close to dying in the darkness.

"And what happens if you fail?" Durmok asked.

Zendric grimaced. "That is why I have asked you to prepare for war. If my efforts bear no fruit, there may be no other—"

A crack loud enough to make Driskoll cover his ears rang out. He looked up to see fissures opening throughout the domed ceiling. Light stabbed through the cracks in thin but growing beams. The people below stared up at the noise and stood frozen. Then someone screamed.

Everyone scrambled from their seats, retreating to the edges of the main chamber as fast as they could. All except the gnome, who stood screaming, paralyzed in terror. Torin leaped from his chair at the head of the table and snatched her from her chair, just as huge chunks of marble tumbled from above, smashing into the floor and sending up a cloud of dust.

"Dad!" Driskoll shouted. He leaned far over the gallery's railing, wondering if he could somehow fly to his father's aid. Almost before he could complete that thought, though, he felt Kellach and Moyra grab him by his elbows and pull him back from the edge. Driskoll turned to protest, but his brother and their friend kept hauling him along, heading straight for the stairs.

"Let go of me!" Driskoll said. "What do you think you're doing?"

"We're not doing anyone any good up here," Kellach said. "We need to get down there now!"

14

CHAPTER

3

When Driskoll, Kellach, and Moyra reached the foyer, Driskoll could barely see a thing. Dust from the falling ceiling billowed out from the main chamber, chasing a stream of screaming people.

Kellach tried to worm his way through the stampede, but Moyra and Driskoll pulled him back before he could be trampled.

"Wait," Moyra said. "Once these cowards leave, we can go in."

"Go, Locky," Kellach said to his dragonet. "Find Dad." The creature's wings clicked open, and he took to the air.

As soon as the foyer cleared, the three sprinted after the dragonet. Dust spilled down from the large hole in the ceiling and Driskoll could hardly see.

"Dad!" he shouted. "Dad!"

Panic shot through him as he tripped over some of the

rubble underfoot and landed hard on a few more fragments of the ceiling. The last he'd seen of his father, he'd been directly under this stuff. How could anyone have survived it?

His eyes started to tear up as he glanced around and realized that the others had gone ahead without him. Although he told himself the tears were because of the dust, he knew better. He and Kellach had lost their mother—the wizard Jourdain, Zendric's greatest student—shortly after the Sundering of the Seal five years back. He couldn't believe fate would be so unkind as to take their father too.

If Torin died, Kellach and Driskoll would be orphans. Who would raise them then? Over the years since his mother's disappearance—perhaps her death, although he'd never let himself believe that—Driskoll had often felt like an orphan. Torin's work as captain of the watch took up almost every one of his waking moments, and Driskoll often went for days barely talking to him.

There had been many nights when Driskoll had wished privately that his father had gone missing instead of his mother. Those had been cold, selfish thoughts, he'd known, but he'd been unable to banish them entirely. When faced with the reality that he might lose Torin, though, those thoughts fled as if set afire. At the moment, Driskoll wanted nothing more than to make sure that his father was not dead.

"Dad!" he yelled again. Desperation scraped his voice rawer than the dust had.

"Over here!" Torin shouted somewhere ahead.

Driskoll tried to put up a cheer, but when he inhaled, a double lungful of dust set him coughing worse than ever.

"Locky found him!" Moyra said from the same direction as Torin. "He's hurt."

"Dad!"

"Stay away, all of you!" Torin shouted. "Get out of here. It's not safe."

The dimness over Driskoll's head began to lighten, and he looked up to see bits of the ceiling still dangling from the edges of where the roof had fallen in. It seemed as if the daylight were beating back the dust, forcing it to settle back into the Town Hall—or at least into Driskoll's lungs. He still couldn't see a thing on the floor around him, though. He could barely see his own shoes.

Where was Kellach in all of this? Or Zendric? If there was ever a time they needed a wizard, it was now, and the only two wizards Driskoll knew seemed to have disappeared.

"Hold it right—you!" Moyra said, still hidden somewhere in the dust.

"Get away from her!" Torin shouted, and Driskoll heard the sharp *hiss-ting*! of a sword being drawn from its scabbard.

"It's not her I'm interested in, old friend," a voice said. "It's you."

The sound of that voice sent a bolt of ice down Driskoll's spine. At once, he knew whom it belonged to, with its unique texture of smooth diction and unmistakable menace.

Lexos. It could only be Lexos.

Driskoll couldn't fathom how the disgraced cleric had escaped his mountain prison. The distant cave had once served as the lair of Gryphyll, one of the creatures after which the Knights of the Silver Dragon had been named. The dragon had sealed Lexos in the place himself before heading off to search for others of his kind. He'd told the Knights they'd never have to worry about Lexos again.

But the dragon had been wrong.

"You can't catch me, you old elf," Moyra said, taunting the cleric. "I'm too young, and you're too slow!"

Driskoll scrambled forward through the dust and over the rubble, almost on his hands and knees, scraping his fingers and legs on the broken rocks. He didn't know what he would find ahead of him. He only knew he had to get there as fast as possible.

A blinding flash of blue-tinged light arced straight across Driskoll's field of vision, burning through the dust. The report nearly deafened him, echoing off the walls of the chamber. The sharp odor of a thunderstorm tickled his nose as he caught his breath and forced himself forward once more.

"You think you can hurt the likes of me with your parlor tricks, my friend?" Lexos said from somewhere to the left. "You have no idea of the power I now wield."

The bolt of lightning seemed to have scorched away some

of the settling dust. Driskoll spied Moyra right before him, crouched over a large, flat stone and pulling at it with all her might. Torin lay with his leg trapped beneath it.

"Dad!" Driskoll said, as he reached his father. Terror grabbed his heart when he saw his father pinned helplessly to the ground with a mad, murderous cleric charging about the place, but he knew he had no time for such things now. Instead, he knelt down and dug his fingers in around the edges of the stone lying on his father's leg. As he did, Locky landed atop the rock, clutching it with his tiny claws and flapping his wings as if he were strong enough to help pull it upward.

"It's not as bad as it looks," Torin said, grimacing. "The stone landed next to me and then toppled over on my leg."

"What happened to the gnome?" Driskoll said, trying to take his father's mind off the pain he had to be in.

"Ran off as soon as the rock hit me." Torin started to curse, then realized that Moyra and his son were listening. He bit his tongue halfway through his words, then gave a weak but sheepish smile. "Sorry," he said. "You were right, Driskoll. You're not kids any more. If you can't hear language like that in a spot like this, then when can you?"

Driskoll wanted to laugh, but pulling on the stone was taking all his breath. Still, he filed his father's words away for later use.

"On three," Moyra said, gritting her teeth. Driskoll knew

she'd heard worse language from Breddo nearly every day of her life. "One, two, three!"

Driskoll heaved that rock, straining with all his might. It seemed it might never budge, but he knew that they didn't have to move it all that much, just enough for his father to be able to remove his leg from beneath it.

Torin screamed so loud and long that Driskoll wanted to call a halt to their efforts. Maybe he and Moyra were doing him more harm than good. But when Driskoll looked into his father's face, he saw not pain but grim determination, and this spurred him into using every last ounce of his strength.

With a lion's roar, Torin yanked his leg from under the rock and rolled away, a red trickle of blood trailing behind him. Driskoll and Moyra let the stone loose, and it slammed into the floor hard enough to shake the building again and knock a few small stones free from the roof.

"Are you all right?" Kellach asked, as he emerged from the last of the settling dust clouds.

"No thanks to you," Driskoll said, putting a shoulder under his father's left arm. "Where were you?"

"Hunting for Lexos," Kellach said, ignoring his brother's irritation as he got under Torin's right arm. The two stood up together and hauled their father to his feet. Lochinvar lifted himself into the air on his wings and flapped out ahead of them, heading for the sunlight outside.

"Did you find him?" Moyra asked.

Kellach nodded, even as his father scowled.

"Now there's a fool's errand," Torin said. "The best thing for most people to do when faced with a man of Lexos's power is run."

"You wouldn't," Kellach said.

"I'm the captain of the watch," Torin said. "It's my job to run toward danger, not away from it."

Moyra glanced down at Torin's battered leg as his sons helped him limp toward the door. "You don't look like you'll be running anywhere for a while," she said.

As Torin and the three kids made it to the entrance to the Town Hall, they spotted Zendric standing at the edge of the terrace, in the center of the top of the wide steps overlooking Main Square.

"Where is he?" Torin called, his voice raw with pain.

Zendric glanced behind him. But before a word could leave his lips, a winged demon swooped down from behind the Town Hall.

The creature looked like a gigantic cousin to the quasit, fat and bloated, its gray-green skin the color of a rotting corpse. With one swift motion, it plucked Zendric off the terrace and hauled him high over Main Square.

Zendric tried to shout something at the demon, but the creature silenced him with a sharp shake of its massive arms. Then the beast winged over a nearby rooftop and disappeared from sight.

Driskoll heard Lexos's mad cackling rolling like thunder over the terrified people huddled behind the booths of the market below.

"Useless people of Curston"—Lexos laughed as he strode up the steps toward the Town Hall—"who will save you now?"

CHAPTER

4

Driskoll stared down the steps at the paunchy man with wild blond hair and icy blue eyes. The slightly pointed tips of the man's ears and his fine features spoke of the elf blood that ran through his veins, but the mad glee that twisted his lips into a gloating sneer ruined his handsomeness.

A scream went up from somewhere near the Great Circle, and then the people in the market started to run. Driskoll watched them streaming out of the square to the north, south, and west, away from the Town Hall as fast as their legs would carry them. The stands in the market stood empty and unguarded, but no thieves stopped to raid them. Even they were too concerned for something far more valuable: their lives.

"Fly, boys," Torin said softly. "Take Moyra with you. This is no fight for you."

"We beat him twice, Dad," Driskoll said. "We can do it again."

"You had help each time, whelp," Lexos said, as he came to a stop on the edge of the steps. "First from Zendric and then from that dragon Gryphyll. Alone, you haven't a prayer."

Kellach pulled away from Torin and began to chant something in a language Driskoll knew he would never understand. Before he could finish his spell, though, Lexos waved a glowing hand at him and said, "Silence, pup!"

Mid-word, Kellach stopped talking, or so it seemed. When Driskoll looked at him more closely, he saw that his brother was still talking. He just couldn't make any noise.

Torin hefted his sword and pointed it at Lexos, who stood there in his blood red robes, laughing.

"I'll bet you wish you could do that around your household, eh, Torin?" Lexos said.

"Stay away from my son." Torin pushed himself free from Driskoll and hobbled toward Lexos.

The cleric raised his eyebrows at the watcher. "Ever the valiant soul," he said with a chuckle. "You could join me, you know. The demons will need a few special souls to help them run this place when they take over. I could put in a few words for you."

"May St. Cuthbert make me the instrument of his retribution," Torin said.

The cleric shook his head in mock pity. "Those aren't quite the words I was thinking of."

Lexos muttered a quick prayer filled with words that made

Driskoll's ears turn red. Then, his hands glowing again, he made a shoving gesture.

Torin flew backward as if knocked down with a giant's club. He hit one of the marble columns in front of the Town Hall with a sharp crack and crumpled to the ground.

"Dad!" Driskoll raced to his father's side.

After all Torin had been through in the past, Driskoll had started to think the man might be invulnerable—not by some magical means, but in the way of the heroes of legend who never seemed to die. Right now, though, Driskoll's faith in that fantasy was torn to pieces. He'd just seen a demon carry Zendric off, presumably to tear out his heart. If the wizard could be killed so casually, then anyone else could die too—including his dad.

"Get away!" Torin shouted as Driskoll came toward him. The watcher's face contorted in pain as he spoke. "Get to safety, now!"

"I'm not leaving you," Driskoll said, as he reached his father. Sweat trickled down Torin's pale face as he squirmed into a sitting position. Driskoll knelt beside him.

Moyra rushed up beside them. "Is he all right?"

Torin looked up at Driskoll. "That's an order, son. Take Moyra with you."

"How sweet," Lexos said. "To be so concerned for your children at the moment of your death. Don't worry, old friend. You'll soon be beyond worrying for them—or anything else."

Lexos began to pray to his evil god again. Driskoll grabbed

HAWTHORNE

his father by the shoulder and tried to haul him to his feet. Even with Moyra helping on the other side, he knew they'd never make it, but they had to try. He couldn't leave his father there to die. He wouldn't let Lexos make an orphan out of him.

Before Lexos could finish his prayer, though, Kellach charged into the cleric from behind and tackled him to the ground. Lochinvar swooped in right behind him, tearing at the old elf with his claws. With the silencing spell cast on Kellach, Lexos hadn't heard him coming. The same spell Lexos had used to nullify Kellach's spells affected the old cleric now too, and the two rolled about on the stone terrace, eerily quiet.

"My pouch," Torin said. "There's a metal vial in it, a healing potion. Get it for me."

Driskoll stared as his father for a moment, stunned. By the time he started to look for the pouch on his father's belt, Moyra had already found it. She tore the wax-covered cork out of the mouth of the vial with her teeth and started to pour it down Torin's throat.

"—for that, pup!"

Driskoll turned to see Kellach rolling across the marble. Lochinvar hovered over his master unsteadily, one of his legs bent out of shape.

Before he knew what he was doing, Driskoll leaped to his feet and charged right for Lexos. He drew his own sword as he ran and held the point out before him.

Despite his growing skill with his sword, Driskoll had never killed a man before. When faced with the choice, he found he usually preferred to threaten force rather than use it. If pushed to action, he tried to wound instead of kill. His father had told Driskoll once that he lacked a "killer instinct."

Right now, as mad and frightened as he was, Driskoll wanted nothing more than to prove his father wrong. He held his sword high above his head in a two-handed grasp, prepared to bring it down and through Lexos with every ounce of strength in his arms. Just as he started to swing his blade, though, the cleric reached out and touched him on the arm.

Driskoll froze solid, as still as a statue. Off balance, his momentum forced him forward. For a moment, he hoped his sword might still strike true, but Lexos stepped to one side and Driskoll toppled face-first onto the floor.

As Driskoll lay there on the cool marble, pain lanced through his cheek. He thought it was unfair that he could still feel everything but not move a muscle. Even his eyelids were stuck open. He couldn't even manage to shed a tear.

Lexos's shadow fell across Driskoll's face.

"How very valiant," Lexos said. "Just like the Knights of the Silver Dragon you and your friends pretend to be. And now you get to share their horrible fate: an early and painful death."

Lexos began to chant. Driskoll struggled inside, hoping he could somehow break the spell. If he could move a finger, wiggle his nose, or even sneeze, he might have a chance. But nothing worked, and his time had just about run out.

Then, despite the cloudless sky, a bolt of lightning arced out and speared the cleric through the chest.

Lexos screamed out and fell to his knees.

Zendric appeared next to the cleric, standing between Lexos and Driskoll, protecting Driskoll with his body. Driskoll's heart beat faster in his frozen chest.

Zendric limped as he moved, and his robes showed long tears along the shoulders. Lexos shook his head in disbelief.

"This madness must end," Zendric said softly. "Curston faces its most dire hour. We need your aid, not your attacks."

The cleric snarled as stood on his knees. "And why do you think you face such travails now? Who do you think might have set the Prophecy of the Dragons in motion? It's all been a sham, you doddering old fool. From the day I first came to town, my thoughts have not been on how to save the city but how to make it my own!"

"You demon-evil dog!" Driskoll shouted. The spell had worn off, and he could finally give voice to the words he'd carried on his lips since he'd first been paralyzed.

Lexos stood up and grasped Zendric with both hands. "I banish thee to the fiery realms of the Abyss! May you burn in Erythnul's blazing embrace for the rest of time!"

Zendric arched an eyebrow. "You dare much, traitor."

Lexos snarled, "This time, there will be no escape for you, no reprieve for your friends, no way to save this accursed town!"

For a moment, Driskoll could have sworn that Zendric smiled. "Lexos, you don't know the powers with which you—!"

"Begone!" Lexos's voice echoed like thunder off the front of the Town Hall and across the abandoned stones of Main Square. "And this time, burn in the Abyss—forever!"

In an instant, Zendric vanished in a fiery puff of brimstone, leaving Lexos standing over Driskoll, his arms clutching nothing but air.

Lexos threw back his head and laughed.

CHAPTER

5

D riskoll clenched the sword in his hand and wiped the sweat from his face. Fear threatened to freeze him as solidly as Lexos's spell had, but desperation forced him forward. Zendric might be gone—maybe even dead—but he couldn't think about that at the moment unless he wanted to share the wizard's fate. He had to do something now, while Lexos's guard was down. It might be his only chance.

"Shut up!" Driskoll shouted, as he stabbed forward at the cleric's heart.

Overjoyed with his triumph over Zendric, Lexos seemed to have forgotten about Driskoll. Driskoll relished the look of surprise on his face as the tip of his blade tore open a hole in the cleric's robes and ripped into his chest.

Unfortunately, Lexos's ribs turned aside the point of the sword. A howl of pain erupted from the cleric's twisted lips.

"You'll pay for that, boy!" Lexos growled, stepping back.

He started to chant, but as he did his eyes grew wide in fear.

Driskoll grinned as he watched Lexos spin on his heel and sprint away toward the south edge of the terrace. Finally, someone—an adult, and an evil villain at that—had shown him some respect.

"Out of the way!" Torin said, as he shouldered his way past Driskoll, charging after the fleeing cleric.

Driskoll's face fell as he realized that Lexos was trying to escape not his blade but his father's.

Despite his disappointment, Driskoll sprinted after his father, hoping to lend a hand. Together, the two of them might be able to corner Lexos and bring him to justice.

As the cleric reached the southern edge of the terrace, which looked out over a twenty-foot drop to the street below, he turned back and snarled at both Torin and Driskoll. "This isn't over," he said. "It's just beginning."

Torin roared and swung his sword at Lexos's neck. Before it bit flesh, though, the cleric disappeared, and the blade cut through nothing but the smoky puff of brimstone left behind.

Torin cursed loud and long. Driskoll wiped his blade on his shirt before sheathing it again. His father has always taught him to keep his weapons clean and sharp, and, given Torin's mood, Driskoll refused to risk refocusing his father's fury on himself.

As the blade rested snug in its home, Driskoll felt a hand on his shoulder. Then he found himself in his father's embrace.

"Are you all right, Driskoll?" Torin's voice trembled with something more than simple anger now.

Driskoll nodded, then whispered, "Yes." He cleared his throat. "I'm not hurt."

"Good," Torin said. "Let's check on your brother and Moyra."

"I'm all right, Dad," Kellach said, his face flushed with shame, his nose already turning black and blue where the cleric had smashed it. Lochinvar perched on his shoulder again, cooing in sympathy at his master's injuries. "I just wish I'd been able to stop him."

Torin gathered Kellach into a strong hug too, tousling his hair as he did. Driskoll noticed his brother had grown over the past year, but he still stood several inches shorter than their father. Torin whispered something into Kellach's ear that made Kellach smile.

"And you, Moyra," Torin said, as he released Kellach from his grasp. "My thanks. If you hadn't gotten me that potion in time . . ."

"It's no problem," Moyra said, blushing. Driskoll knew she didn't much care for his father, mostly because Torin kept catching her own father and putting him in jail. Still, she basked in his approval as much as the boys did.

Gwinton raced up the stairs with a platoon of watchers behind him, his battle-axe in his hand. The red-faced dwarf grimaced at his commander as he snapped him a salute.

"Report," Torin said, all business again.

"I'm sorry, sir. We were busy evacuating the crowd, keeping the cowards from trampling one another to death. If we'd known you were still in the—"

"Don't worry about that now, Gwinton. Report."

Torin kept his tone even and casual. He'd allowed himself a moment to curse fate when Lexos had escaped, but now he was the eye within the storm, still and calm while all whirled about him. Driskoll could see why his father had been named captain of the watch, and he wondered if he could ever be so cool in the face of such pressure.

"We got most of the people out of the Town Hall, sir, and gathered in the Great Circle, near the bottom of the obelisk." The dwarf stabbed a stubby finger at the white-marble pillar poking out of the clear area that the tents and stands of the bazaar surrounded.

"Take five watchers and search the hall for survivors and bodies," Torin said. "And be careful. What's left of the roof may not be stable yet."

"Right away, sir."

"A moment, Gwinton." The dwarf stopped himself in the middle of turning away.

"Did Latislav make it?" Torin asked.

The dwarf nodded. "He's in the Great Circle. He wanted to minister to the wounded, but the worse anyone there has is a scrape or two."

"Send Tarrel to fetch him. My sons could use some of his attention."

Gwinton glanced at the boys and then nodded firmly. "Right away, sir."

Gwinton turned to address Tarrel—a tall, thin watcher who couldn't have been much older than Kellach—but the young watcher had already left to find Latislav.

"Dismissed," Torin said.

The dwarf didn't move.

"Sir?" Gwinton said.

"Spit it out, watcher," Torin said.

"What happened, well . . ." He thumbed his axe for a moment. "What about Zendric?"

Driskoll's gut fell as he considered the wizard's fate. Getting away from a murderous demon was one thing. Coming back from the Abyss, where Lexos had banished him, that was a whole different trick. The Abyss was the home of all the demons that had tortured Curston during the Sundering of the Seal. Could even Zendric stand against an entire realm filled with such monsters?

Torin grimaced. "I'm afraid we'll have to find our way without him the best we can. We lost many of our best after the Sundering of the Seal, and we survived that. We'll do so again."

Gwinton nodded firmly and pointed at five of the other watchers in turn. "You lot are with me. The rest of you, back to your duties. We can't have every watcher in town wandering

35

around Main Square, especially with Lexos lurking about. Now, go!"

As the other watchers dashed off to fulfill their orders, Tarrel arrived with the blue-robed, old cleric in tow. "I found him on his way here," the young watcher told Torin.

The captain dismissed Tarrel with a nod of his head. Before he could explain what he needed to Latislav, the old man had already started to examine Driskoll and Kellach.

"I'm fine," Driskoll said, as the cleric looked him over.

"It never hurts to be sure," Latislav said, leaning hard on his gnarled staff as he peered down at Driskoll's face. "But I think you're right. Your brother, on the other hand, has a broken nose."

"I'll be okay," Kellach said. "Save your prayers for the people in the Town Hall. They might need them more."

The old man chuckled as he set down his staff. "I think St. Cuthbert can spare a bit of his favor for such a brave lad. Hold still for a moment."

As Latislav murmured, his hands began to glow with a golden light. He placed his hands over Kellach's face, and the glow flowed from his fingers into Kellach's battered nose. When Latislav removed his bony hands, he smiled at Kellach and asked, "Now, how's that?"

Kellach wriggled his nose. "Much better, thanks."

Latislav patted Kellach on the shoulder, then bent over and retrieved his staff. "Excellent. Now I'd better follow Gwinton into the Town Hall. As you say, there may be others there who need the blessings of St. Cuthbert."

Driskoll held a hand over the bruise on his face. Although it hurt, he refused to complain about it while others might be suffering far worse.

"All right, boys," Torin said. "Let's get you home."

"What about Zendric?" Driskoll asked.

Torin grimaced. "I'm sorry, son, but I'm afraid he's gone."

Driskoll struggled not to cry as Kellach glared up at his father.

"You're wrong!" Kellach said. "Zendric is the best wizard in Curston. If anyone can find his way back from wherever Lexos has sent him, it's Zendric."

"I hope you're right." Torin put his arms over the shoulders of both his sons.

Driskoll looked up at his father. "What about Lexos?"

"The watch will scour the city for Lexos until he's found," Torin said as he steered the boys toward their home in the Phoenix Quarter.

"Let's hope they find him soon," said Moyra, tagging along behind them. "He sounded like he wanted to bring us all to the end of the world."

CHAPTER

6

"You're to stay here," Torin said, as he stood in front of the door leading out of his home.

Driskoll scowled as he slumped down in one of the stuffed chairs near the hearth. He hated being stuck in the house, and he knew Kellach did too. The two of them spent as much time outside of it as they could.

Perhaps the place just reminded them too much of Jourdain and the life they once had with her before the Sundering. It had grown dirtier and dingier over the years, and none of them had bothered to do anything to stop its long slide into slovenliness.

"Didn't we just help you drive off Lexos?" Kellach asked, looking up from the scratched and dinged table where he'd been working to fix Lochinvar's bent leg. An everburning torch hanging from a thin length of chain flickered over his head, illuminating the tabletop and casting his face in shadow as he turned to face his father. "This isn't fair."

Torin frowned. "This isn't about being fair, son. It's about you listening to me for once."

"But, Dad—" Driskoll started. He had a whole argument prepared about how they were getting older now and deserved to be treated with some more respect.

"You think I don't know about how you two sneak out of here at all hours of the night to go on your little adventures? I am the captain of the watch. I catch criminals more clever than you every day." At this, he shot a glance at Moyra. "How stupid do you think I am?"

"Dad!" Driskoll said. "Even Zendric trusts us to handle things on our own these days."

"He is not your father. I am."

"Remember when that demon posing as Mom had everyone in town eating out of her hand?" Kellach asked. "Who stopped her then?"

"That woman—!" Torin thundered, then cut himself off. When he spoke again, he forced his tone to be calm. "That creature that posed as your mother desecrated her memory. You are not to mention her again. Not in this house."

Thinking back, Driskoll realized that the last time he'd seen his father happy was when Nahemah had been impersonating Jourdain, when they'd all thought they'd had Mom back for good—and not all of that had been due to her magic. Torin missed his wife more than he cared to share with his

39

sons. Driskoll knew that it weighed on him every day. Today, it seemed like a millstone around his neck.

No one spoke. For a moment, it looked like Moyra might say something, but Kellach shot her a look that made her bite her tongue.

"I know you're getting older," Torin said. "I know you deserve more responsibility. I didn't object when Zendric wanted to make you Knights of the Silver Dragon, even though I knew what that would lead to. I haven't locked you in your room or posted a watcher around the house to keep you in."

Torin stopped again and then gazed deep into each of his sons' eyes. "Don't you see? Most of the time, I let you go on your crazy adventures. I don't barge into your room when I hear Moyra climbing in through your window. I don't keep your sword or your spellbook under lock and key. Most of the time, I figure whatever trouble you get into you can get out of.

"This time is different though. This is about the Prophecy of the Dragons. And if it comes true, Curston could well become the first outpost in the Abyss's renewed war on our world. So, now more than any other time in your lives, I insist you listen to me and stay here!"

Driskoll looked to Kellach, who frowned at him then nodded. "All right, Dad," Kellach said. "We'll listen."

Moyra started to say something again, but once more Kellach silenced her with a dirty look. She groaned and sat down on her hands in one of the parlor chairs.

"Thank you." Torin exhaled as if he'd been holding his breath all day long. Then he strode over to the dining table and reached out to pluck Lochinvar from between Kellach's hands. "But just to make sure, I'm going to place your pet here under house arrest too."

"What?" Kellach shoved himself away from the table, disgust and anger warring on his face. "Don't you trust us?"

Torin grimaced. "I love you, Kellach," he said, as he walked over to a silver cage hanging from a chain in the back corner of the room. "But trust is something you earn. It's not given back so easily to those who abuse it."

"You can't do this," Kellach said, flushing with anger. "Locky isn't yours. He's mine."

Lochinvar didn't protest as Torin slipped him into the cage and closed the filigreed silver door behind him. "And you're my son. You live in my house."

Torin took out a tiny silver key hanging from a chain around his neck and locked the cage's door with it.

"I'll leave then," Kellach said. "I'll go live with Zendric."

"Who do you think gave me this cage?" Torin asked, as he slipped the chain and the key back under his shirt. He looked over at Moyra, who still hadn't said a word. "Don't bother trying to pick it. Even your father couldn't open this lock."

Moyra glared at Torin.

He came over and looked her straight in the eyes as he spoke. "I've known you since you were born. I've known your parents

41

for much longer than that. Breddo and I were close once, just as you are with my sons."

Driskoll had never heard this before. From the look on Moyra's face, it was news to her as well.

"Let me give you a bit of heartfelt advice," Torin said. "Don't follow in your father's footsteps. They only lead to prison and pain."

Moyra screwed up her lips and spat in Torin's face. "You're not my father," she said, as the watcher straightened up and wiped his cheek clean.

Torin glared down at the girl, and for a moment Driskoll feared he might slap her. Instead, he headed for the door. As he reached it, he looked back at them all.

"Stay here," he said. "If I find you on the streets, I'll have you tossed into Breddo's favorite cell." Then he stormed out of the house and slammed the door behind him.

Locky chewed on the bars of his cage. Moyra stood up and cursed.

"Hey," Driskoll said. "That's our father."

She spun on him, her red hair flaring out behind her. "Did you hear what he said about my dad?"

Driskoll shrugged half-heartedly. "Sure, but still."

She narrowed her eyes, then stalked over to Lochinvar's cage to examine the lock on its door.

"We need to get out of here," Kellach said. "Now."

Driskoll stared at his brother. "Didn't you just tell Dad

you'd stay here—and then ask him to trust you?"

Kellach growled in frustration. "That was before he stuck Locky in a cage."

"You mean before that you still meant to stay here while Zendric is dead and all of Curston falls to pieces around us?"

"Stop being so annoying," Kellach said. "First, Zendric is not dead. He's missing. Second, if we don't get out of here soon, Dad will send a watcher to stand guard over the house. He's that mad. We have to leave before that happens."

Over at the cage, Moyra cursed Torin again. "He's right," she said. "Zendric did something magical to this cage. Only a wizard could open it."

Locky stopped gnawing on the bars around him long enough to growl in agreement.

"A powerful wizard, she means," said Kellach, as he walked over to look at the cage. "If Zendric put a spell on this cage to keep in Locky, you can be sure he made it too strong for me to do anything about it."

"Can't we just break it open?" Driskoll said.

Kellach ran a hand over the cage's silver bars. Lochinvar nuzzled his fingers with the tip of his metallic nose.

"The cage is reinforced with magic. Even if we stole snips from a blacksmith's shop, we wouldn't be able to scratch the metal. If we use anything less precise than that, we might hurt Locky."

"So we're leaving him here?"

"We have to," said Moyra. "Even if the snips might work, Kellach's right. We'd come back to find a squad of watchers waiting for us."

Kellach nodded as he poked two fingers through the bars of the cage to stroke Lochinvar's cold, hard skin. "He'll be safe here," he said. "That's more than you can say for us."

Driskoll put his hand on the hilt of his sword. "Where are we going?" Dread filled his heart as the image of Zendric being consumed by a cloud of brimstone flashed before his eyes.

Kellach looked at his brother and Moyra, a smile spreading on his face. Driskoll knew that, despite fighting with Torin about it, his brother actually looked forward to this adventure; it was another chance to test himself, to prove he was on track to become the great wizard he hoped to be someday.

"We're going to look for Zendric," Kellach said, already heading for the door.

CHAPTER

7

"S o, tell me again," Driskoll said, as they opened the creaky door that led into Zendric's stone-walled tower. "What exactly are we looking for?"

"I'm not sure," Kellach said, as he strode into the place like he owned it. In a sense, Driskoll thought, this was his brother's second home. If you took away the hours he slept, Kellach spent more time here than he did at his real home.

Kellach had shown some aptitude for magic, so Zendric had taken him under his wing and made him his apprentice. Although the two sometimes butted heads, they'd grown to care about and even respect each other. More than once, Driskoll had heard Zendric call Kellach his most promising student—better even than Jourdain.

"Zendric?" Moyra called out. "Anyone home?"

Driskoll and Kellach stared at her. Driskoll hadn't imagined that the wizard might be here, safe and sound. Now that he thought about it, he wanted nothing more. They all waited a moment for a reply. But none came.

Driskoll's heart felt like it might shatter. Kellach glared at Moyra.

"What?" she said with a half-hearted shrug. "If he escaped, where do you think he'd go first?"

Driskoll shook his head. To lose Zendric at any time would be horrible. For him to be gone now, when they needed him most, was a disaster.

"Did you see Lexos after Zendric disappeared?" Driskoll said. "I don't think he's coming back any time soon."

Kellach grunted, clearly not ready to accept facts yet. "If anyone could prove Lexos wrong, it would be Zendric. Don't count him out yet."

"I wasn't . . . ," Driskoll started to explain , but he couldn't come up with any words that wouldn't make it sound worse. Besides, he admitted to himself, he had counted the wizard out.

"Never mind," he muttered.

Driskoll joined the others, peering around the place. The fact that they didn't know what they were looking for never came up. Driskoll knew that they'd recognize it when they found it.

Unlike some of the other towers in town, Zendric's place was not round but square. The wizard normally held lessons and entertained visitors on the first floor. A number of desks stood shoved against one wall, parchment and inkpots covering them, some neater than others.

"The spiritkeeper is missing," Moyra said from where she stood near the fireplace. "It's not on the mantel anymore."

Driskoll remembered the magical device from when they'd saved Zendric's life for the first time. Someone had used it to steal Zendric's soul, and it had been up to the three of them to track it down and restore Zendric's spirit to his lifeless body. They'd unmasked Lexos as the culprit behind it all, for which Driskoll was sure the ex-magistrate would never forgive them.

"It's upstairs in his workspace now," Kellach said. "Zendric decided against keeping it in such a public place."

Moyra nodded. "Smart."

"Let's head up there," Kellach said. "Zendric never keeps anything all that interesting down here any more."

Driskoll and Moyra followed Kellach up the stairs along the back wall. As they went, Driskoll took care to stay far away from the railing atop the banister, which was carved to resemble a large, venomous snake. He knew Zendric had put it there to scare off unwise intruders, but it still bothered him to even look at it.

Upstairs, Zendric's workspace was messier than usual. Scrolls of parchment had been pulled from the shelves along one of the walls and unfurled across nearly every spare inch of floor. Books lay scattered atop them, many stuffed with carved wooden placeholders and notes scribbled on bits of scrap paper. An inkpot had been overturned in the corner, but it seemed there had been no ink in it.

"What was he working on?" Moyra asked, as she uncovered one of the everburning torches placed in sconces throughout the room. The heatless flames on these never went out, but they shed enough light to read by, even on the darkest night. "A spell for duplicating books?"

"The Prophecy of the Dragons," Kellach said, as he pored over a stack of notes covering a writing desk that stood against the wall between a pair of windows overlooking the street below.

"Did he tell you anything about it?" Driskoll said, as he read a few of the gilt titles on the nearest bookshelf. *Zagyg's Sources of Greyhawk, Rekab's Eberron Gazetteer, The Good Knight's Guide to Lancing Dragons* by Hicks and Weisman, *Doowneerg's Mnemonics for Remembering Realms*, and so on.

Kellach shook his head. "It's here."

"What?" Moyra and Driskoll snapped their heads around to stare at Kellach.

"It's here." Kellach ran a hand over the top sheet of parchment on the desk before him. "This is what Zendric was working on."

The two others rushed to Kellach's side. Driskoll peered at the writing scribbled on the parchment in front of them and realized he couldn't read a word of it.

"What language is that?"

"Draconic," Kellach said. "Most wizards keep their notes in it. Zendric says it's good practice for when you're copying spells."

48

"Can you read it?" Moyra asked.

"Most of it. It doesn't all make sense to me though."

"I thought you knew Draconic." Driskoll couldn't resist the chance to needle his brother a bit.

"I've never seen some of these words before. I think I can make out most of it though."

"What's it say?" Moyra asked, giving Driskoll a little shove for bothering his brother on purpose.

"Hold on a minute." Kellach stared at the parchment for a long time. Driskoll noticed his lips moving but resisted the temptation to say something about it.

"It's something about the Sundering of the Seal. This isn't the whole thing, I don't think, just a part of the prophecy that Zendric copied down here to analyze closer.

"It mentions how the demons will attack from the Abyss and be held back by the ones willing to make 'the ultimate sacrifice.' But their efforts won't be enough. Eventually, their repair of the Seal is doomed to fail unless . . . "

Driskoll and Moyra waited patiently for Kellach to continue. After what seemed like a lifetime, Driskoll said, "Unless what?"

"Sorry." Kellach shook his head and unfurrowed his brow. "Unless we find and use the Key of Order. Only then can the Seal be remade permanently."

"What?" Moyra said. "Why hasn't Zendric done this already?"

"Maybe he doesn't have the Key of Order," Driskoll said.

Kellach shuffled through the pieces of parchment. "Wait a minute." He looked at the first few pages and put them aside, one by one. On the fifth page, he stopped and started to read in earnest.

"He had it," Kellach said. "He had it and used it when a group of treasure hunters broke the Seal the first time. It didn't go well."

"I guess not," Moyra said sarcastically. "We still can't go out at night around here without worrying about having our heads torn off."

"It says here that centuries ago, a band of heroes cleared out the Dungeons of Doom, trying to make the region safe for the good people that lived here. When they reached the lower levels, they found a magical gate that led directly into the Abyss, the home of the demons that still plague us today. The heroes used a powerful artifact known as the Key of Order—forged in platinum to resemble a dragon—to create the Seal over the gate. This put an end to the demonic infestation.

"The heroes then founded Promise nearby and created the Knights of the Silver Dragon to keep it safe. One of the heroes—a wizard who specialized in divination magic—created the Prophecy of the Dragons to warn future citizens of Promise of the dangers the Dungeons would once again pose to them someday.

"Over the years, other monsters moved into the Dungeons."

"Why not?" said Driskoll. "Lairs aplenty and no waiting."

"When there were enough monsters around, a new generation of adventurers—treasure hunters, really—decided to roust them out too. One such group found the Seal. Thinking of the dungeons—and treasure—that could be behind it, they broke it."

"That was the Sundering of the Seal?" Moyra said.

Kellach nodded. "It had been so long since the Seal had been created that most everyone had forgotten about it. Nearly all of the original Knights of the Silver Dragon had died by then, and other people had taken their place. Of the original order, only Zendric was left."

Moyra pursed her lips. "He's been here since the beginning, and now he's gone. There's only us left to carry on."

The weight of that responsibility hung on Driskoll like a leaden harness. He felt himself start to hyperventilate.

"He believed in us," Kellach said, putting an arm around his brother. "I think he hoped this day wouldn't come so soon—that we'd be older and more prepared when it did—but here it is. We have to face it."

Driskoll nodded and swallowed hard, forcing the fear back down into the bottom of his belly. He knew it would still gnaw at him from there, but at least he'd gotten it out of his head and his lungs.

"Is there more?" Moyra said, pointing at the papers.

Kellach nodded. "Zendric and the handful of Knights he

still had around then fought their way into the Dungeons of Doom and made it down to where the broken Seal stood. When they tried to use the Key of Order, though, it failed. It broke into three pieces."

"How did they manage to seal it then?" Driskoll asked. "I mean, even partially?"

"According to this, they pieced it together with their bare hands," Kellach said. "It didn't work as well as it would have, but it was enough to re-create most of the Seal—enough to keep the worst of the demons at bay. But . . . "

Driskoll stared at his brother as his eyes scanned the bottom of the parchment in front of him again and again. Tears welled up in Kellach's eyes, and his cheeks flushed red.

"What?" Moyra said in a hushed tone. "What is it?"

"There's a list of the last Knights of the Silver Dragon right here." Kellach's voice was so raw that it surprised Driskoll he could speak at all.

"Who's on it?" Driskoll asked, almost certain he didn't want to know the answer.

"There are a dozen names," Kellach said, pointing at the symbols along the page. "This one up here is Lexos's. The last three are Torin, Breddo, and Jourdain."

CHAPTER

8

Y ou're . . . ," Driskoll stared at his brother with raw eyes of his own. He took a deep breath before he spoke again. "You're not joking. I knew about Mom, but Dad?"

Moyra's lips curled into a frown. "My dad?" she said. "He was a Knight too? How come no one ever told me about this?"

Kellach bowed his head. "Zendric once told me that most of the Knights were killed in the battles after the Sundering of the Seal. It seems that those that survived gave back their pins."

Driskoll's hand went up to the silver dragon pin on his own chest. Touching it calmed him, helped him to find his center. The thought that his father might have worn that very pin comforted him.

"Those were dark days," Kellach said, "even before the Sundering of the Seal. It's possible the Knights of the Silver Dragon had become a secret order by then. Your mother may not even have known about Breddo being a Knight."

Eager to change the subject, Driskoll spoke up. "So what happened to the Key of Order?"

"Yeah," said Moyra. "And if the Prophecy of the Dragons says it can be used to repair the Seal, why did it fail?"

"I don't know," Kellach said. "These notes don't say why, but I think that's why Zendric hasn't tried to use it for the past five years. It must have been too dangerous to try."

Driskoll scratched his chin. "But at the meeting in the Town Hall, Zendric said he was ready to use it now."

Kellach nodded as he read further down the page. "That's how bad things are. This says that if the Key of Order fails a second time, it could destroy the Seal entirely. There would be nothing stopping the demons from coming through. If you think that quasit we saw this morning was nasty, you should see his bigger cousins."

Moyra shook her head. "We have to try it. We have to find the Key and try to repair the Seal."

Kellach nodded. "If we don't, no one else will. Dad and the watchers are too busy protecting the town. Zendric's gone. It's up to us."

"This is insane," Driskoll said. He felt like he might vomit at any moment.

"You're not going to make us put this to a vote, are you?" Kellach said.

Driskoll shook his head. "No. You're right. I just don't want you to be."

"So," said Moyra, "where can we start to look?"

"According to these notes, Zendric scattered the pieces of the Key of Order throughout Curston. He wanted to make sure no one could just take it and use it."

"Is one of them here?" Driskoll asked.

Kellach raised his eyebrows and pursed his lips. "It stands to reason. If you had to protect something like a piece of the key, it would make sense to leave it with the most powerful wizard in the city."

"What are we waiting for?" Moyra said. "Let's turn this place over."

"Hold on," said Kellach. "There's more here. Zendric gave two of the pieces to the 'most loyal' and 'most faithful' people in Curston, it says."

"That means the remaining piece *must* be here," Driskoll said, his voice cracking with excitement.

"Let's find it, quick!" Moyra said.

The three of them set to poking around the library bit by bit, piece by piece. They took every book and scroll off the shelves, opened them, and put them back, one by one.

"Be careful," Kellach said. "Zendric has all sorts of dangerous things around here. You don't want to trigger something by accident."

Driskoll, who was holding a glass jar filled with a viscous red fluid and sealed with wax, scoffed. Then something in the fluid squirmed. Driskoll yelped and bobbled the jar. The jar

55

slipped from his fingers. Driskoll grabbed hold of it again just before it fell and shattered on the floor.

"I said, 'Be careful,'" Kellach said. "We don't want to make things worse than they are."

"I think they might already be," said Moyra, who stood peering out the window. "Look!"

Driskoll carefully set the jar back down exactly where he'd found it and then dashed over to the window. On the street outside, a handful of masked, armed men strode toward Zendric's tower.

"Who are they?" Driskoll asked.

"Thieves," Moyra said. "Here to rob the tower."

"What?" said Kellach. "How do you know that?"

Moyra shot him a look as she padded over to the door that led downstairs and knelt next to it. "I know thieves," she said. "People don't wear masks in the middle of the day if they're up to something good.

"Lexos got rid of Zendric in front of everyone in Main Square too. That means the whole town knows about it. Someone had to wonder if there might be something worth taking here now that Zendric's not around to protect it."

Someone knocked at the door downstairs.

"Maybe we should answer it," said Driskoll. "If they know someone's here, they might go away."

Moyra shook her head. "Anyone who wears a mask in broad daylight like that isn't going to be scared off by three kids."

"Could we lock the door before they get in?" Kellach asked.

"I did that when we walked in," Moyra said, cocking her head to listen down the stairs. "But it won't stop them."

The boys stood next to Moyra and cocked their heads like hers. Driskoll heard the sound of metal scraping on metal, and then the door opened with a long, aching creak.

"The coast is clear," a muffled voice said through a mask. "Spread out and keep your eyes peeled. Don't touch anything you don't have to though. Anything in this place might be trapped."

"I thought a 'master thief' like you could take care of those," another voice said.

"Not if you trip them first," the first voice said. "And we don't have the time. If we've figured out this angle, you can be sure others will try to get in on the action soon. Best to be here and gone before that happens."

A third voice, rough and raw, laughed. "Most'll be too scared to come here before dusk and then too scared too walk the streets. This plan is foolproof."

The first voice spoke low and bitterly, "You're a fool to think so."

"We have to stop them," Kellach whispered. "We can't let them just wander through here and take whatever they want."

"How are we going to do that?" Moyra asked. "Just go down there and ask them to leave?"

"Maybe we can just lock ourselves in here," Driskoll said. "Then the worst they can do is trash the first floor."

"Did you see how fast they picked the lock on the front door?" Moyra said. "The one on this door isn't half as good. Even if we jam it up from the inside, they'll just break down the door, and then we're doomed. They outnumber us five to three, and they're much bigger."

Kellach stepped back from the door and started to chant something softly. Then he reached up and grabbed his throat with both hands.

Driskoll stepped aside as Kellach walked over to the door. He didn't bother to be quiet this time. In fact, he stomped about as if he wanted the thieves to hear him.

"Who goes there?" Kellach called down the stairs in a voice that was not his own. It took Driskoll a moment to place it, but then he knew. It was Zendric's.

"Who dares enter my abode uninvited?" Kellach said, louder this time.

"Abode?" Moyra whispered.

Driskoll just shrugged. He was used to hearing Kellach flex his vocabulary, and he suspected his brother was enjoying having a good excuse to try it.

"Gods!" a voice downstairs said. "He's here!"

"Hold it," another voice—the first one, again—said. "Let's not be so hasty."

"You can stand here and argue with the wizard about

whether he's back or not," a voice said. "I'm not about to stick around to see who wins that one."

The front door creaked open again. Driskoll padded over to the window and peered out to the street below. There he saw the masked men trotting away.

"It worked!" Driskoll said. "You did it!"

Moyra jumped up from where she knelt and gave Kellach a big hug. "I can't believe it," she said. "What morons!"

"Hey," Kellach said, as he walked back into the center of the room. "It was a good spell, well cast. It would have fooled anyone."

"Well, most people, anyhow." A man stood in the doorway, staring at the three kids through an old sack that covered his face, except where someone had cut holes for the eyes. It reminded Driskoll of the head of a scarecrow that he'd seen on a trip to a farm last summer, except that now the eyes weren't stitched in with black thread.

"Just as I suspected," the man said. "The time for games here is over."

CHAPTER

9

The man reached up and untied the cord that held his mask fast. Then he pulled the makeshift hood from his head and flashed a wide smile.

Sweat matted his curly, sandy hair to his head, and concern danced in his sparkling green eyes, but there was no mistaking who it was.

"Daddy!" Moyra said, leaping into his arms.

Breddo dropped the mask and caught his daughter in a big bear hug. After a moment, Breddo said with a grin, "Baby, I think you're getting a bit too big for me to carry around."

Moyra jumped off of her father, her smile mirroring his own. He held her at arm's length and looked her over from head to toe.

"You're not hurt, are you?" Breddo said. "I wasn't in Main Square this morning, but I heard all about it."

Moyra shook her head. "The boys took the worst of it."

Breddo looked at Kellach's nose and then winced at the scrapes and bruises Driskoll still showed.

"Sir." The suspicious tone of Kellach's voice warned Driskoll what was coming. "What were you doing with those thieves down there?"

Breddo glanced at the ground. He scooped up his mask and stuffed it into his pocket, a sheepish look on his face. "Ah, yes. I thought you might be wondering about that. Perhaps we should retire downstairs so I can explain myself."

Breddo held his arms wide to allow the kids to precede him down the stairs. Kellach went first, and Driskoll saw him looking back as he descended, making sure that Breddo was right behind them.

"So?" Kellach said to Breddo.

"Well, as I suppose you've already figured out, I was here to secure the place against undesirables. Seeing as how Zendric was removed from our fair city so abruptly, I conjectured that his home might need an extra bit of protection from those who might take advantage of the situation to prey on his belongings."

Driskoll coughed. Hard.

"Do you have a cold?" Moyra said, a vicious edge in her voice. "Maybe you ought to go home."

Driskoll rolled his eyes. "You can't possibly—"

Moyra stopped him with a deadly sneer. "You can't possibly want to question the honor of a fellow Knight of the Silver

Dragon." As she said these last words, she walked over and put her arm around her father's waist.

Breddo looked down at his daughter and gave her a nervous smile. "Ah, so you've found out about that, have you?"

She nodded up at him with a smile on her face.

"Well," Breddo said, looking away, "that was a long time ago."

Moyra looked up at her father for a moment, then withdrew from him and folded her arms across her chest. Driskoll wanted to hug her then, but he thought she might punch him if he tried.

"Anyhow," Breddo said, "the question is not, apparently, what I'm doing here, but what you lot are here for?"

"We came to see if we could find something here to help us find Zendric," Kellach said. Driskoll noticed that Moyra hadn't even tried to speak.

"And did you find anything?"

"Do you know about the Key of Order?"

Breddo's eyes opened wide, and he let out a long sigh before nodding. "So, it's come to that, has it?" He glanced around the inside of the tower. "Old friend, we could use you now."

"Zendric's notes mentioned that the Key broke into three pieces. We need to find them and reassemble the Key so we can fix the Seal."

Breddo gaped. "I can see why he chose you three to be the first of his new knights. You're all barking mad."

"Daddy!" Moyra stomped away from her father and sat down in a chair in front of one of the desks shoved up against the far wall.

"If we don't do this, the Prophecy of the Dragons makes it clear that the patch placed over the Seal will soon give way. When that happens, demons from the Abyss will have free access to the city."

Breddo nodded. "Poor Curston won't last a week." He looked over at his daughter. "Isn't there any other choice?"

Moyra refused to meet her father's eyes.

"No," Breddo said softly. "Of course there isn't."

The man walked over and put an arm around his daughter. Despite how angry she was, she leaned into him, putting her head on his chest. With one hand, he stroked her reddish hair.

"I've been a fool," Breddo said. "A selfish, short-sighted fool. Ever since the Knights of the Silver Dragon broke up and, well, since Jourdain disappeared, I've . . . "

He frowned and let out a long breath. "Let's just say I've not been the man I once hoped I'd be."

Moyra wrapped her arms around her father's chest. When she pulled her face away, Driskoll saw patches of dampness on his shirt.

Driskoll didn't think he'd ever seen Moyra cry before, even like this, so softly he couldn't even hear her weep. Zendric's disappearance and Lexos's triumph must have affected her more than Driskoll had thought. The notion that someone as strong and tough as Moyra was so shaken made him more scared than ever.

"But that's in the past," Breddo said. "The city needs us now, so it's time to rise to the call, whoever we may be. Let's find that Key."

Kellach smiled. "Zendric's notes say he gave away two of the pieces of the Key, one to the most faithful and one to the most loyal."

"I suppose that counts me out," Breddo said, tousling Moyra's hair as he did. She grinned up at him. "Where's the other one then?" he asked.

"My guess is that Zendric hid one of the pieces here in his home," Kellach said. "Where else would be safer?"

Breddo nodded. "Of course. Smart lad."

The three kids resumed their search of the place, this time with Breddo at their side. Before he joined in, though, he went to the front door and shut and locked it.

"Just to make sure we won't be disturbed," he said. "Only a handful of people in Curston could pick a lock like that, and two of them are right here." He smiled at Moyra, who blushed.

"I was surprised there wasn't some sort of spell in place to keep people out," Driskoll said.

"Sometimes, lad, a wizard relies more on his reputation than his spells to maintain his privacy."

The four turned everything in the tower upside down, one

piece at a time. At one point, Moyra found the spiritkeeper, hidden in the back of a trunk filled with rune-covered papers.

"Should we take it with us?" she asked. "I mean, just in case?"

"Put it back where it was," Kellach said. "If we need it later, we'll know where it is."

"If someone had told me that thing had been crushed to a thousand pieces, I wouldn't shed a tear," Driskoll said. He still had nightmares about the day they'd had to track that artifact down to save Zendric's life.

Then his eyes fell on the silver dragon statue sitting on Zendric's mantel. "Hey," he said as he reached for it, "wasn't this thing in a thousand pieces the last time I saw it?"

"Fixing it would be a simple spell," Kellach said.

"For you?"

"For Zendric."

Kellach peered over Driskoll's shoulder as he examined the statue. "It's hollow. Zendric kept the Knights of the Silver Dragon pins in it, remember?"

Driskoll felt for the pin on his chest as he thought about that. There had been dozens of pins hidden in the statue. If there had been one for each Knight of the Silver Dragon, how many of them had there been? And what had happened to them all? For that matter, whose pin did he have now?

"I think the head comes off," Moyra said.

Driskoll held the statue's body tight, grasped its snout tight, and then wrenched it to the left. It screwed off at the neck, and after a few turns, the head came off in his hand.

Driskoll walked over to a low table near the large, stuffed chair in which Zendric often sat while giving his lessons. He turned the statue over, and the pins inside spilled out on to the table.

Breddo gasped at the sight. "So many," he said softly.

"Would you like one, Daddy?" Moyra asked.

The man winced at the suggestion. "I would like nothing better, baby, but I think it's best if I don't. If we do find Zendric and he sees me wearing one of those pins, I'd probably wish we hadn't found him."

"Can I see that?" Kellach said to Driskoll, pointing at the body of the statue.

Driskoll handed it to his brother, who brought it up close to the light of an everburning torch nearby. Kellach tapped various parts of it with the nail on his index finger, listening carefully. Contented, he smiled, then smashed the statue on the tabletop.

"What in the Abyss are you doing?" Driskoll asked, as he leaped back from the flying shards of pottery.

"Finding part of the Key of Order, I think."

Kellach swept much of the ruined statue to the floor. This left behind a large, flattish piece that had sat in the front of the statue, seeming to be the dragon's underside, stretching from its neck to its tail and even along its limbs.

"It's platinum," Breddo said. "Old Zendric must have had the statue molded around it."

"Is it what we've been looking for, though?" Moyra asked.

Then everything went black.

CHAPTER

10

The entire room plunged into darkness as if the darkest night had fallen over Curston in an instant. Driskoll couldn't see the back of his hand, nor even the everburning torches that supposedly never went out.

"Get down!" Breddo said.

Only magic could make the room so dark, Driskoll knew. Otherwise, he'd be able to see the light coming in through the tower's windows. As it was, he might as well have been blind. But who would barge into Zendric's home and start throwing around spells like this?

"Lexos!" he said. "It has to be Lexos."

"Very clever, boy," the cleric's voice said somewhere in the blackness.

A noise came from the table on which the piece of the Key of Order lay, and then a yelp that could only have been from Moyra.

"Traitorous slime!" Breddo shouted.

Then the door opened and slammed shut.

Driskoll charged for the door and ran into someone else—someone who grunted just like Kellach. He threw himself back to let his brother past, but stumbled into him again at the door.

"It's locked!" Kellach said.

"From the inside?" Moyra asked. Driskoll sighed in relief at the sound of her voice.

"Magically, I think."

"I'm after him," Breddo said. "You lads get my girl home safe!"

"Wait!" Moyra said, but her father didn't stop.

Driskoll heard him taking the stairs to the second floor two at a time, with Moyra's footsteps right behind.

Driskoll went after them, feeling his way up along the opposite wall, still avoiding the snake-banister as best he could.

When Driskoll reached the second floor of the tower, he could see again, although the room below him was still steeped in blackness. He saw Moyra standing at one of the windows that faced the street.

"He's gone," she said, as she turned around, her face flushed.

"Can you see him?" Kellach said, coming up behind Driskoll.

Moyra shook her head. "He's too fast. The best second-story man in town, he always said."

"Think he can catch Lexos?" Driskoll asked, peering out the other window. A few people strolled down the street below, but he saw no sign of either man.

"If anyone could, it would be him . . . but, no." Moyra's voice sounded funny, and when Driskoll pulled his head back in through the window, he saw she had her face buried in her hands.

He knew what she was thinking. He felt like bashing his head against the wall himself.

"Some Knights of the Silver Dragon we make," Kellach said, disappointment tainting his tone. "We might as well have just handed Lexos the Key of Order."

"Don't be so hard on us," Driskoll said. "Lexos was here before us, probably looking for the Key himself. When he heard us opening the door, he must have found a way to become invisible or enter the astral plane or—anyway, how he hid from us isn't important, just that it would have been almost impossible for us to find him, even if we'd known he was there."

"How do you know that?" Moyra said, a bit of hope in her voice.

Kellach sucked at his teeth. "Driskoll's right. Zendric wouldn't have left the place unprotected by magic. The reason we didn't run into any was because Lexos had already used his own spells to get rid of it."

"So he just waited for us to find the part of the Key hidden here so he could take it from us." Moyra said. A smile cracked through her gloom. "Well played." Driskoll heard a hint of admiration in her voice.

"I should have figured it out," Kellach said, smashing a fist into Zendric's desk. A crystal paperweight sitting there fell from the surface and smashed on the floor, shattering into tiny shards. "I'm such an idiot!"

Moyra and Kellach stared at the ruined paperweight and then at Kellach. Driskoll wondered if the paperweight had been something valuable and magical, perhaps another spiritkeeper. He waited for something horrible to take place, an evil soul to swirl out of the scattered shards, but nothing happened.

"It's okay," Moyra said, putting a hand on Kellach's shoulder as he slumped over the desk, quivering with either anger or shame—or both.

Driskoll wanted to say something, but he couldn't think what. He'd never seen his brother like this. Kellach exuded confidence. When Kellach got backed into a corner, he only became surer of himself, and most of the time—to Driskoll's eternal irritation—he was right.

To see Kellach frustrated like this shook Driskoll to the core. He wanted nothing more than to tell his brother everything would be all right, but that was the way of children. If being a Knight of the Silver Dragon had taught Driskoll nothing else, it's that they were far from being children any more.

"There are still two other pieces of the Key of Order out there," Driskoll said. His voice came out raw and strained, nothing like what he had hoped for. He cleared his throat and tried again, this time speaking strong and clear. "We just need to get to them before he does."

"Why?" asked Moyra. "We need all three to fix the Seal. We're never going to get that first one back from Lexos."

Kellach straightened up from the desk and nodded at Driskoll. "If he wants it that bad, he might have some use for it beyond just stopping us. We need to make sure he doesn't find the other pieces." He looked at Moyra. "Unless, of course, you want us to take you home like your father asked."

She scowled at him. "Where to then, apprentice?"

Kellach rubbed his chin for a moment. He'd developed the barest shadow of a beard there, and Driskoll knew his brother hoped to one day have long whiskers to stroke while he pondered such questions. For the moment, at least, everything seemed normal again.

"I got it," he said, turning on his heel and starting for the stairs.

Moyra and Driskoll fell into step behind Kellach. As they made their way to the door, Driskoll realized he could see just fine down here. Whatever Lexos had done to cause the darkness had worn off.

"Where are we going?" Moyra said, as they hit the street.

Kellach strode off toward the center of town with a mission

to his step. "The Cathedral of St. Cuthbert."

Driskoll almost tripped. Instead he stumbled into the trot he used to catch up with his longer-legged brother. "Why?"

"Where else are we going to find the most faithful man in town?"

"Latislav?" Moyra said. "More like the dullest."

"He may not be the preacher Lexos was when he ran the church, but hey, he never tried to kill us."

"Why not one of the moneylenders?" Moyra said. "They have the best safes in town, strapped to their roofs and beyond."

Kellach shook his head. "It would have to be someone Zendric knew, someone he trusted. He used to trust Lexos—before that thing with the spiritkeeper. He trusts Latislav too."

"Maybe Zendric's not the best judge of character," Moyra said.

"That's not the point. We have to figure out who he trusted and who had the power to keep these things safe. My money's on the cathedral."

"All right," Driskoll said, grudgingly accepting his brother's argument. "So where's the third piece?"

"With the most loyal person in Curston," Kellach said.

"Your dad," Moyra said. "The other piece must be in Watchers' Hall. It has dozens of watchers running in and out of it twenty-four hours a day. There's no better place in town to keep something safe."

"What about the Curston Treasury?" Driskoll asked. "Wouldn't that be a safer home for a piece of the key?"

Kellach snorted. "We broke into that place."

"You make it sound like that was easy."

"Breddo himself couldn't break out of the jail under Watchers' Hall. Moyra's right. Zendric gave Dad one of the parts of the Key. He was a Knight of the Silver Dragon, after all. Who else would he trust?"

"There were a lot of names on that list. A lot of pins in that statue."

"Trust me," Kellach said. "Think about it. Trust your gut."

Driskoll frowned. They made a lot of sense. The worst part was that Driskoll didn't have any better answers himself.

"So why are we going to the cathedral first? Dad would be a lot easier to talk to about this than Latislav."

"It's on the way to Watchers' Hall. Besides, we're supposed to be sitting safe at home."

"Ah, right."

They fell silent as they reached Main Square via the north entrance. The cathedral loomed over the place from the west, most of the hundreds of people in the bazaar ignoring it out of habit. They only paid attention to the place when it rang the starting and ending bells for the town's curfew.

Stabbing upward from the steeple atop the church's bell tower, the ruby-crusted, circled cross of St. Cuthbert glared

74

down over the square, hunting for Lexos, it seemed, or any other traitors like him. The scandal with Lexos trying to kill Zendric had shaken the church to its roots—and its believers' faith along with it. The people who still worked there—including Latislav—seemed determined to do everything they could to clean that horrible blot from the town's memory. From the bare trickle of petitioners flowing through the cathedral's doors, even during the highest masses, it seemed they still had a long way to go.

The sun stood high in the sky, beating down on Main Square. As they walked past the obelisk in the center of the Great Circle, Driskoll noted that its shadow pointed toward noon.

No stalls squatted in the Great Circle, the edges of which were lined with rocks with silver seams, but many people stood there, chatting with friends or chewing on their lunches. The smell of food wafting over from a nearby tent made Driskoll's mouth water, but he knew better than to try to call a halt to fill his body now. There would be time for a meal later, he hoped.

As Driskoll strode past the outer limit of the Great Circle once again, he felt the world grow a shade darker. As Kellach had explained to him and Moyra months ago—it seemed almost like a lifetime now—the circle wasn't just the largest sundial anyone had seen. It had been enchanted to keep out demons and other evil creatures too. Such beasts could not cross the silvery lines.

Driskoll wondered how many people could fit inside the Great Circle should the worst happen. A hundred? A thousand? What would happen to anyone unfortunate enough to not reach the circle in time? And how long would the demons be able to keep the good people of Curston trapped in the circle? Would they persist until the citizens ran out of food and water, their circle an island in a sea of evil? Or would they find some other way to kill everyone inside it long before that?

"Wait," Moyra said, as they climbed the well-worn steps up to the cathedral's front door. There, under a bas-relief scene that depicted St. Cuthbert himself slaying a demon, she grabbed the boys' arms and pulled them toward her. "What if this is another trap that Lexos has set for us? How do we know he's not following us around invisibly again?"

"We don't," said Kellach.

"Don't you have a spell or something you could use?" Moyra asked.

"Not really." Kellach bowed his head for a moment. Driskoll could tell he wanted so much to be a better wizard right then, one at the prime of his career instead of the beginning. "Lexos's spells are far more powerful than mine. Even if I could come up with the right spell on the spot—which I can't—he'd probably still be able to mask his presence."

"He's not here," Driskoll said.

"How do you know that?" Moyra asked.

"If Lexos knew there was a part of the Key of Order here,

he'd have claimed it a long time ago. He was in charge of the cathedral for years. He'd have known right where the piece was, and he'd just take it before anyone could stop him."

Moyra and Kellach stared at Driskoll for a moment. He felt his heart drop. No one except his brother and their best friend ever listened to him. Were they going to stop doing that too?

"Good point," Moyra nodded. She spun and trotted up the last few stairs to pull open one of the smaller doors set into the twenty-foot-tall ironbound double doors that looked out over the stairs.

After being in the sunlit Main Square, the inside of the church seemed as dark as a tomb. It took a moment for Driskoll's blinking eyes to adjust. When they did, he saw Moyra already ahead of Kellach and him, charging up the main aisle to talk to the man kneeling in front of the large, wooden altar at the head of the room.

The nave of the church—the great hall in which the people worshipped St. Cuthbert during services held here—felt like a vast cave. The vaulted ceiling hung so high over Driskoll's head that he could barely see it in the shadows. The main aisle ran between rows of polished pews that faced the altar at the far end of the nave, which stood far enough away that Driskoll thought he might not be able to hit it with a bowshot. The sweet scent of burning incense filled the air, its smoke hanging over the candle-lit altar like a cloudy halo.

"Latislav?" Moyra called out.

The cleric knelt with his back to the aisle, before an array of votive candles arranged around and on top of the altar.

"Yes, daughter?" The old man took his staff from where it rested on the dais, on which the altar stood, and used the gnarled length of wood to push himself to his feet. Driskoll swore he could hear his joints creaking from halfway down the church's center aisle. "What can I do for the three young heroes who helped drive off Lexos this morning?"

"We're looking for a part of the Key of Order. We think it might be here."

"Really?" The old cleric raised his bushy eyebrows. "What makes you think that?"

"That's not important," Kellach said. "We just need to know where it is. Now."

Latislav was famous for taking forever to complete a sermon much less come to a decision. Driskoll breathed a sigh of relief that his brother wasn't willing to tolerate that right now.

Neither of them had managed to sit through a whole of Latislav's services without falling asleep, and as far as Driskoll knew Moyra had never set foot in the cathedral—at least not to attend services. Fortunately, Torin wasn't much of a churchgoer, and he rarely compelled his boys to go to church with him. They'd never gone alone.

Latislav inclined his head. "Do you happen to know what this part of yours looks like?"

Kellach glanced at the others before answering, but they

were no help at all. "We think it may resemble a silver dragon," he said. "It would look like either its head or its wings. We've already seen its body."

"About how large?" the cleric asked.

Kellach held his index finger and thumb apart. "That much maybe. It's hard to tell."

"Yes, yes, yes." Latislav rubbed his bare chin for a while, his eyes unfocused, and gazed at the rosette window at the back of the Cathedral.

"So," Driskoll said, expecting some sort of eloquent response after all that thinking.

"So?" Latislav said.

"Do you know where we could find something like that?"

"Something like what?"

Driskoll groaned in frustration.

"Where is the part of the Key of Order that resembles a dragon's head or wings?" Kellach said.

"Oh, that," Latislav said with a smile, which made Driskoll wonder if the cleric was faking the memory loss for fun or was really on the edge of becoming a doddering old fool. "Yes, of course. I know exactly where something like that is."

CHAPTER

11

"Follow me, children," Latislav said, crooking one withered finger.

Driskoll, Moyra, and Kellach followed the elderly cleric, who seemed to move at a snail's pace, even with the help of his staff as a walking stick. Driskoll imagined that if all the demons of the Abyss came knocking on the cathedral's front door, Latislav would still walk down the aisles of the church at the same exasperating pace.

The four of them proceeded in silence as Latislav led the way to the left of the altar and behind it into a space cut off from the nave by a set of heavy tapestries. The weavings on these depicted epic scenes from the mortal life of St. Cuthbert on his way to becoming the god of retribution, the one that more people in Curston worshipped than any other.

In the wider world, there were more gods than Driskoll could count. It seemed like the elves, dwarves, halflings, gnomes, and so on each had their own pantheon too, some of which Driskoll couldn't distinguish from their human counterparts other than by their appearance.

Driskoll wondered if in fact there was just one god, and the people of Curston worshipped many different aspects of it. But then he thought about gods like Erythnul, the god of slaughter whom Lexos now worshipped, and he couldn't understand how Erythnul could be part of the same deity as St. Cuthbert.

For that matter, how could Lexos switch from being the high cleric of a good god to one who valued only evil? Perhaps the line between retribution and slaughter was a bit too fine, something you could wander over when you weren't paying attention. Or maybe that nebulous difference made it easier for a man who'd always harbored evil in his heart to show the face of goodness.

"Here we are," Latislav said, jarring Driskoll from his reverie. Once behind the tapestries, the cleric had led them up a tight spiral staircase to a wide, shallow room that ran across the short end of the nave, overlooking the altar far below through a wooden screen. Driskoll realized he'd probably glanced up at the screen every time he'd been in the place and never once wondered what might be behind it.

The room stood bare but for a number of artifacts and religious icons collected in display cases around the three sides of the room. A frieze, taken from another, older building, topped the back wall and was lit from beneath with everburning torches, which Latislav patiently uncapped, one by one. A pair of laminated wooden screens that showed the ascension of St. Cuthbert into godhood stood against one of the shorter walls. On the wall opposite, a set of shelves displayed various bits and pieces collected from St. Cuthbert's life. A dark-stained cudgel served as the centerpiece, with all sorts of other weapons arrayed around it.

"There it is." Kellach stood staring at something on a shelf to the left: a dagger with a serrated edge. It seemed sharp enough to cut even their eyes if they gazed on it for too long. Still, Driskoll saw at once what Kellach was excited about.

The handle of the knife was a silver dragon's head, open wide as if ready to savage a foe with its bite. Sapphires twinkled in its eye sockets like winter stars. Driskoll wondered who would dare hold such a thing in battle.

Latislav reached over and picked up the knife. "Precisely what I thought you might be referring to, son," he said to Kellach. "This is one of the rarest knives in this realm or any other. It once belonged to St. Cuthbert himself. Although he was known for carrying a cudgel, of course, he sometimes needed a blade close to hand, and this was the one he favored."

Moyra peered over Driskoll's shoulder. "Did it always look like this?"

The cleric raised his eyebrows at the girl. "Why, no," he said. "How very peculiar that you should know that.

"Before the Sundering of the Seal, the handle of this knife

was carved from the wing of a demon that St. Cuthbert slew with his own hands. When the Seal was broken, those in St. Cuthbert's service used everything they had to help defend the city. That included this knife."

Latislav glanced at the walls around them. "Five years ago, shelves of weapons from St. Cuthbert and his greatest followers filled this room. Many of them were lost or destroyed in the battle that followed the Sundering of the Seal. Even this knife . . . " He hefted the weapon in his hand. "The handle of this knife was shattered. Someone—Zendric, I believe—replaced it with this casting of a silver dragon's head. I think it was his way of remembering all of the Knights of the Silver Dragon who died in that battle."

"We need it," Kellach said.

Latislav smiled wide, a look of serene understanding on his face. "Why?"

Kellach pointed at the dragon's head. "This is part of the Key of Order, an ancient artifact that can be used to repair the Seal in the Dungeons of Doom."

"I say we destroy it," Moyra said. "Right here and now."

Latislav gasped as if the girl had stabbed him through the belly. "Why in the heavens would you wish to do that?"

"Lexos has one of the other pieces."

"He just grabbed that to stop us," Driskoll said.

Moyra shook her head. "I've been thinking about it. If that's the case, why steal the body piece? Why not just destroy it? I think he wants the Key for himself—all of it."

"And why would that be?" Latislav said.

"So he can destroy the Seal entirely," Kellach said, his face deadly serious. He looked around at the others and then back at the knife. "It stands to reason. If the Key of Order can lock the Seal up tight, then it can unlock it too."

"So we can't risk that," Moyra said. "We have to destroy it."

"But that means we won't be able to restore the Seal either. Eventually it'll just give way, and it'll be just as bad as if Lexos had undone the Seal himself."

"That could take years," Moyra said. "Decades."

"Or it could happen tomorrow," Latislav said. Driskoll nearly jumped, having counted the old cleric out of the conversation.

Kellach nodded and put out his hand for the knife. "So we have to destroy it."

Latislav smiled again as he grasped the handle of the knife tighter. "I'm afraid not. This is an artifact of St. Cuthbert, and it is my sworn duty to protect it."

Kellach cocked his head at the cleric. "We don't need to destroy the knife, just the handle."

"The two are now as one as far as the Church of St. Cuthbert is concerned. When the new handle replaced the old, it was blessed with the same reverence as the original. To destroy it would be an affront to St. Cuthbert. The god of retribution could not let such an offense pass."

Moyra stepped toward the cleric. "This is more impor-
tant than maybe hurting your god's petty feelings," she said.
"We're talking about saving every man, woman, and child in
Curston."

"Including a lot of his worshippers," Driskoll chipped in.

"The answer is no," Latislav said. "I suggest you find the
third part of this Key of Order and do with it as you like. This
sacred dagger will remain here, safe and unharmed."

Moyra's hand snapped out and tried to snatch the weapon
from the cleric. As she did, he moved just enough so that her
fingers closed on the edges of the blade instead.

"Ouch!" Moyra said, plucking back her hand. She stuck
a finger in her mouth and sucked on it as she glared at the
cleric.

"I think you should leave," the cleric said, putting his staff
between himself and the others. "Now."

When the three kids stood their ground, the cleric spoke
again. "I am older than all of you put together, and that may
make me a tired, old man. I am still, however, the high cleric of
St. Cuthbert in Curston, master of this sacred cathedral.

"I am not without power of my own. If you try to take this
knife from this building or to destroy it—whether by guile or
brute force—I will stop you. If I fail at that, I will follow the
exacting tenets of my religion and hunt you down and make
you pay for your blasphemous affront."

"I vote we take it," Moyra said, never taking her eyes from

85

the cleric. Blood dripped from her cut finger.

"I vote we respect the cleric's wishes," Kellach said.

"Well," Latislav said to Driskoll. "As I don't believe I'm allowed a vote in your new order, I think it's up to you."

12

I can't believe we didn't just take it from him!" Moyra growled as they left the cathedral.

"We put it to a vote," Driskoll said. He couldn't keep the irritation out of his voice.

"I can't believe you voted against taking it from him!"

Driskoll exploded. "Forgive me for thinking that knocking over an old man—who could probably kill us all with a single prayer to St. Cuthbert—and stealing something from him was a bad idea!"

Kellach put a hand on Driskoll's shoulder to calm him down. "Hey, I voted against taking it too."

"That's right!" Driskoll said to Moyra. "It was two against one. You lost. Live with it."

"So you're both idiots!" Moyra said. She made a fist at Driskoll, and for a moment he thought she might hit him. Then she grunted, "Ow!" and she stuck her hurt finger back on her mouth.

87

"Hey," Driskoll said, pulling her finger out of her mouth and staring at the wound. "I just voted not to take it from him then. We'll go see if we can find thre one in Watchers' Hall." The cut was superficial, but Driskoll didn't doubt it hurt. "If not, we can always come back to the cathedral and take it when Latislav's not around."

"Seriously?" she said with a note of hope.

"I didn't mean to vote against you so much as delay the decision," he said. "It just didn't make sense to start a fight with Latislav there and then. The demons of the Abyss are our common foe. If we can't unite against them, we're all doomed."

"Where's Kellach?" Moyra asked, glancing about.

Driskoll hadn't noticed his brother leaving them alone in front of the cathedral. He scanned the crowd of stalls and people stretching out in both directions along the front the cathedral, and spotted Kellach standing in front of a stand selling roasted chestnuts.

Kellach paid the vendor and strolled back over to the others. "Open your pocket," he said to Driskoll, holding up a small cloth filled with chestnuts.

When Driskoll did, Kellach poured the chestnuts into his brother's pocket. They felt warm and solid through the thin lining of his pocket, which nearly brimmed over.

Kellach took the cloth that had held the chestnuts and flapped it about until it was clean. Then he tenderly wrapped it around

Moyra's cut finger and tied it tight. "Hold that gently," he said. "The pressure should keep it from bleeding, and the wrapping should help keep the cut clean."

Moyra nodded at Kellach but didn't say a word. Driskoll saw the gratitude in her eyes.

"Have some of the nuts," Kellach said, as he started walking toward Watchers' Hall. "I could hear your stomachs growling the whole time we were in the cathedral."

Driskoll grinned at Moyra as he passed her a handful of chestnuts, which she took in her good hand. She bit into one of the meaty nuts and smiled back.

"Thanks," Driskoll said to his brother. "Of course, salty snacks like this make me—"

A small waterskin arced back over Kellach's shoulder at his brother. Driskoll managed to catch it without dropping any of the chestnuts in his hand.

"Thanks," he mumbled around a mouthful of chestnuts.

Kellach just looked back over his shoulder and winked.

For a moment, while he had food and water at hand and a clear, sunny sky above, Driskoll could forget all about the troubles of the day. He could pretend that Zendric was still home and safe in his tower, deep in preparations for protecting the city from whatever the world—or worlds beyond—might throw at it. He could believe everything could be all right in the end.

Then he spotted his father walking toward them through the crowd milling about the market, and one of the chestnuts he'd been chewing got lodged in his throat.

He spun about and dodged between the two nearest tents, coughing as hard as he could. Kellach and Moyra followed after him as he wove his way past and around a few other stalls until he was sure they were out of Torin's path.

When Driskoll finally stopped, he had nearly turned blue from not being able to breathe.

"What do you think you're doing?" Moyra said. "We haven't got time to pick you up a sandwich too."

Kellach peered at him and saw Driskoll's eyes bulging out as he grasped at his own throat. "He's choking!" he said.

"Oh, gods," Moyra said. "What do we do?" She smacked Kellach on the arm with her bad hand. "Ow! Don't just stand there. Cast a spell or something!"

Kellach reached his arm around his little brother and started to pound him on the back. He hit so hard that Driskoll wondered whether he'd pass out first from the choking or the beating. One of the blows knocked something loose. The piece of chestnut came flying out of his throat and he could breathe again.

"What happened?" Kellach said, concern etched on his face. "You haven't done that since you were in diapers."

"It was Dad," Driskoll said. "I saw him coming straight at us."

Moyra craned her neck all around, hunting for any sign of Torin. "He must have gone past by now," she said. "I don't see him at all."

"This is great," Kellach said with a grin.

"What?" Driskoll said. "That I almost died, or that Dad almost caught us and then would have killed us all?"

"The second one," Kellach said. "I was worried we'd have a hard time getting into Watchers' Hall with him around. Now, the coast is clear."

Driskoll shook his head as Kellach helped him to his feet. "You sure have a strange definition of 'great.' " He rubbed his throat, still feeling the impression the chestnut had made inside him.

"Let's get going then," Moyra said. "Just because your dad's out of the hall right now doesn't mean he will be for long. We may not have much time."

Kellach took off after Moyra as she led the way through the crowd, holding Driskoll's arm. Soon they reached Watchers' Hall and walked straight in.

"You just missed him, boys," Sergeant Guffy said, as they strolled up to the duty desk in the hall's foyer. "He had a meeting, but he should be back soon."

"Can we wait for him in his office?" Kellach said. "It's nothing important."

"Sure thing," Guffy said with a grin. He got up from the desk and hobbled over on his crutch. The tubby, old man had lost the leg to a werewolf in the battles after the Sundering of the Seal. He may not have been a Knight of the Silver Dragon, but from everything Driskoll had heard he'd fought just as valiantly.

"Thanks, Guffy," Kellach said with true affection for the

man that he and Driskoll had known since they were born. Guffy was one of Torin's few remaining friends, and he and his wife had their family over for dinner at least once a month, if only to get Torin to concentrate on something other than work for a while and spend some time with his sons and his friend.

Once they were seated safely in Torin's office with the door closed behind them, Driskoll spoke, "Do you have any idea where the third part of the Key of Order is, or are we just here to make it easier for Dad to find us when he figures out we're not home anymore?"

Kellach nodded. "I did, but it's not here." He stared at a blank space on the wall behind Torin's desk, which seemed to have drowned in a sea of unfurled scrolls. "It used to hang right there."

"What are you talking about?" Driskoll said. "The only thing that ever hung there was a sculpture of the official coat of arms of Curston."

"Which is?" Kellach sat down in the chair behind Torin's desk and began to rub his temples.

"A silver dragon on an azure field," Moyra said. "I never got much schooling, and even I know that."

"Right, and what are we looking for?"

Driskoll smacked himself on the forehead. "Parts of a key made to look like a silver dragon."

"Right. We've found a head and a body so far. What's missing?"

"The wings!" Moyra said.

Kellach smiled.

"But Dad hasn't had that sculpture up for a year," Driskoll said.

"Hm." Kellach leaned forward and put his elbows on the desk. "Has it been that long?"

"At least."

Kellach slid out of his father's chair and walked to the door. Driskoll slipped behind him. "Guffy?" Kellach called out after cracking the door a foot. "Do you know where that coat of arms is? The one that used to hang over the desk?"

Guffy called back down the hall, "Now there's something I haven't thought about in forever. I think your father put it in his closet."

"Really?" Kellach said, surprised. "Thanks!" He shut the door again and strode over to the door of a closet on the far side of the room. It opened easily, and there, on the floor, sat the Curston coat of arms.

Kellach pulled the coat of arms from the closet and carried it over to Torin's desk. As he looked at it, he cursed.

The wings were missing.

CHAPTER

13

The office door opened, and all three of the friends jumped. Guffy stuck in his head, and Driskoll—who'd been expecting his father—let out a long breath he hadn't realized he'd been holding.

"Pity about that, isn't it?" Guffy said. "It was a nice piece."

"What happened to it?" Moyra asked.

Guffy shrugged. "One morning we came in, and the wings were missing. Torin said he thought some thief with more skill than sense must have nicked them." At this, Driskoll and Kellach looked at Moyra. "Torin put it in the closet, and I guess we forgot about it—until now."

Kellach stared at the coat of arms for a moment. "Where did you say our father was?"

"I didn't," Guffy said with a smile. "But since you ask, he's at the cathedral, meeting with Latislav about this whole thing with Lexos."

Kellach bolted from the room.

Driskoll glanced once at Moyra, and the two chased after him.

"Good to see you again too!" Guffy called after them.

On the street, Driskoll and Moyra had to sprint to catch up with Kellach. His robes slowed him down just a bit, but it was enough for the others to gain on him.

Just as they reached Main Square, Moyra—who was by far the fastest of them—managed to grab Kellach by the back of his robes.

"Let go!" Kellach said, whirling around and snatching his robes away.

"What's the big hurry?" Driskoll said.

"Weren't you listening? Dad's in the cathedral."

Moyra nodded and spoke to Kellach slowly, as if he was a small child. "Sure. He's probably talking with Latislav right now—who's sure to tell him we were just there and might even mention how we assaulted him."

Driskoll's eyes widened. "We should be running home right now, so we can be there when he comes back. Otherwise, he's going to kill us."

Kellach sighed at his brother. "The Seal might be destroyed, and all you can think about is whether Dad's going to be mad." He thrust a finger up at the cathedral. "The third piece of the Key of Order once sat in that coat of arms in Dad's office. He might have it on him right now. If so, the two things that Lexos wants most are both in that cathedral right now."

Driskoll turned to look at the cathedral's massive doors and almost choked again. He didn't relish the thought of having to go back in and face Latislav so soon after they'd considered taking the piece of the Key of Order from him. At the moment, he wished to see his father even less.

But they had no choice.

"All right," he said. Moyra clapped him on the shoulder as he spoke. "Let's go."

They walked up the cathedral's steps side by side. When they got to the smaller door set inside the massive ones, it stood open. Kellach went through first, then Moyra.

Driskoll brought up the rear, glancing back at the sunlit square behind him before he plunged into the relative darkness of the cathedral. He longed for something or someone out there to pull him back at the last second, to spare him from having to face Latislav and Torin, but fate chose not to intervene, and he followed the others inside.

As the three walked down the main aisle in the nave, it seemed as if not a single person but them breathed in the place. Then Driskoll heard the voices from somewhere high above and before them. He looked up and saw lights flickering behind the screenlike wall that fronted the room of the church's artifacts.

"Stay away from him, I tell you! Stay away!" The voice

belonged to Latislav, but Driskoll had never heard him sound so desperate.

"By the power of St. Cuthbert of the Cudgel, I banish you from his house of worship. Never dare you to darken his house of worship again!"

The three kids took off at a flat run toward the altar. They slipped behind the tapestries there and charged up the spiral stairs beyond. When they reached the room above, they found Latislav there on his knees, leaning on his staff as he bent over a body, his back to them.

"Did you get him?" Moyra asked, as she led the way into the room.

Latislav's shoulders shook for a moment. Then he turned around, his face flushed red.

"No," he whispered. "I was too slow, too late. And I'm afraid you three are as well."

The cleric pulled himself to his creaking knees and stepped aside. There in front of them, his limbs arranged at uncomfortable angles, lay Torin in his watcher's uniform.

"No!" Driskoll drew back while Kellach dashed forward. He watched as his older brother knelt down to examine their father. Moyra put an arm around Driskoll, giving him a sidelong hug.

"Is he dead?" Driskoll asked. Despite his best efforts, his voice trembled.

Because Torin served as the captain of the watch, Driskoll

had always known there might come a day when his father perished in the line of duty. Every morning, Driskoll made sure to peek into Torin's bedroom, just to make sure he'd made it home that night. Sometimes, Torin's job kept him away for a full day or two at a time. During those times, Driskoll worried the most. Add all of those horrible days together, though, and they didn't add up to how Driskoll felt right now.

"He's breathing," Kellach said.

Driskoll wanted to fall over in relief, but Moyra propped him up.

"What happened?" Kellach said.

Driskoll recognized that tone. His father used it every time he caught Kellach or him doing something wrong. When Driskoll heard it, he knew he'd better have the right answers right away or he'd regret it. This time, though, he had nothing to fear. Kellach spoke only to Latislav.

The cleric leaned against one of the shelves filled with St. Cuthbert's artifacts, his face sweaty and his hands trembling. Twice he started to talk but could not find the words.

Kellach stood up over his father's unconscious body and repeated himself, stabbing each word at the cleric. "What happened?"

"Lexos," Latislav said. "It was Lexos."

"Is he—?"

"Gone," the cleric said, wiping the sweat from his forehead. He grimaced. "I never saw him . . . "

"Start from the beginning," Driskoll said. He kept his voice even and friendly, to contrast Kellach's. Being this upset, the cleric might clam up if he thought everyone in the room was against him.

Latislav swallowed hard, nodded, then tried again. "Torin—your father, boys—came in here to ask me about the part of the Key of Order. He knew right where it was. He grabbed the knife and said he was confiscating it in the interests of the entire town. When I refused to let him, he got angry with me and started shouting.

"Maybe that's why we didn't hear Lexos come in. There I was, arguing with your father, and suddenly he fell over. It wasn't until then that I noticed Lexos in the room with us.

"He came over and took the knife from Torin's hand, laughing at me all the while. That's when I got angry and began to threaten him. He ignored me for a while and then dared me to do something—anything.

"I prepared a spell to cast him out of this place, but before I could bring it off he disappeared. Right before my eyes. Nothing left of him but the air where he'd once been.

"You came in soon after that. Perhaps he left because he heard you on the stairs. He certainly didn't seem to fear me in the least."

Latislav hung his head at these last words. Kellach stared at him hard, unimpressed.

"What did he do to my father?"

The cleric shrugged. "Lexos has grown in power in the service of his new, dark god. His command of divine magic far outstrips my own. In all the city, I thought that perhaps only Zendric could challenge him. Sadly, it seems I was wrong."

"Will he live?" Driskoll asked.

Kellach shot his little brother a murderous look. Driskoll cringed at having vocalized the greatest fear they both had, but he couldn't repress his curiosity any longer. He had to know.

"I should think so, son," Latislav said. "Before he left, Lexos said something like, 'Soon you shall both bear witness to my revenge.' The dead witness nothing, of course."

"Did Lexos get both of the pieces of the Key of Order?" Moyra asked.

Latislav's brow creased as he leaned on his staff. "I'm afraid I don't understand your question."

"He took the knife from you," Kellach said. "Did he take anything from my father?"

"He may have," Latislav said. "Once your father fell, he rifled through all his pockets. He took something from him, I think, although I didn't see what it was."

"And you let him?" Driskoll asked, surprised at how the thought of his helpless father being ransacked enraged him.

"I'm afraid so," Latislav said, his face red with shame.

"He must have all three pieces," Kellach said. "We have to stop him."

"How?" Moyra said. "I thought once he got them all there was nothing we could do."

"He still hasn't used them yet. There might still be time to stop him."

"How can you tell?" Driskoll asked.

Kellach looked around the room. "Curston isn't choking on demons—yet."

CHAPTER

14

W here are you going?" Latislav shouted through the screen wall. Moyra, Driskoll, and Kellach had bolted from the upper room and were already halfway toward the cathedral's entrance. They ignored him.

"Don't do it!" the cleric shouted, as he rapped his staff against the screen. "It will be your death for sure! St. Cuthbert cannot protect you outside these city walls!"

"He hasn't done much of a job inside them," Moyra said.

"It's too dangerous!"

"Hold it," Kellach said, raising a hand for the others to stop. He turned and shouted back up at the cleric, whose shadowy silhouette was visible through the screen.

"Come with us!" Kellach called out. "If it's as dangerous as you say, we could use the help."

"The Dungeons of Doom are too dangerous for anyone." Latislav's voice trembled from far more than his age. "Even if you somehow manage to avoid all the horrible creatures between you and the Seal, buried deep in the Dungeons' darkest depths, you would still have to contend with Lexos."

"We can take him," Moyra said. "We've done it before, and we can do it again."

"If it were a contest of confidence, I'm sure that you would," Latislav said, as he mastered his nerves. "But I fear that will not be enough."

"Better to try than to wait here for the demons to come and slaughter us all," Driskoll said.

"Perhaps," the old man said softly.

Kellach put a hand on his brother's shoulder, and the three of them walked out into Main Square without another word.

"Straight to the Dungeons of Doom then?" Moyra said as she squinted at the afternoon sun.

"Home first," Kellach said, already stumping down the steps. "There are some things there that we need to pick up, but we must move fast. We don't have much time if we want to get there before Lexos."

• • ▮ • •

In minutes, they burst into the boys' home. As they entered, Driskoll found himself hoping his father would somehow be there, waiting to scold them for having left the place. Even though he knew this could not happen, the absence of Torin still disappointed him.

"Grab our packs," Kellach said. "I'll get some food and water. No telling how long we'll be there." He turned to Moyra. "Do you need to go home for anything?"

"Got some rope?" she asked.

Driskoll rolled his eyes at her. "Where's yours?" he asked. "I thought your dad said you shouldn't leave home without it."

"Curston's home. We're leaving. We can go grab the coil at my house if you like, but that will only hold us up more."

"I'm going," Driskoll said, raising his hands in surrender. He raced upstairs and gathered the emergency backpacks he and Kellach kept stuffed under their beds. He checked the oil in their lanterns to make sure they were topped off—double-checked for the length of rope in his pack—and then headed back downstairs again.

"Ready?" Moyra asked. She waited near the door, tapping her foot as she did.

Kellach stood in the far corner of the room, between the two bookshelves. He had reached a finger into the silver cage hanging there and was stroking the dragonet's metallic skin.

"What about Locky?" Driskoll asked.

"It's a well-made prison," Kellach said with a note of sadness. "He's not going anywhere."

Driskoll didn't like the idea of setting out on such a dangerous mission without Locky. He'd gotten so used to having the little guy around that he hadn't realized how much they'd all come to rely on him. Without Locky scouting things out ahead, they might stumble into an ambush—or worse.

"Anyhow," Kellach said, as he snatched his pack from Driskoll and headed for the door, "we're off."

Driskoll thought perhaps he'd seen a tear in his brother's eye. If so, he managed not to point it out.

Soon, the trio reached the ironbound doors of the Westgate. These stood open at this time of day, letting travelers of all sorts pass through the forty-foot stone wall that surrounded the city. Eagle-eyed watchers looked down on the crowd from atop the wall and from stations at either side of the road, scanning the visitors and those departing for signs of trouble, demonic or otherwise.

"Think Dad told them to be on the lookout for us?" Driskoll said.

"I'm sure he had more important things to warn them about—like the demons managing to sneak in." Kellach didn't sound as convinced as Driskoll wanted him to be.

They walked alongside a merchant's wagon on its way out of the city to parts unknown, and its bulk shielded them from at least one of the watchers at ground level. The other didn't pay any attention to them, and the ones above didn't recognize them either—or at least didn't mind. After all, many citizens of Curston took a walk outside the walls from time to time, just to stretch their legs and avoid getting "town fever."

Once outside Curston's walls, the three continued on the main road for about a mile, then turned north on a pathway overgrown with weeds and tall grasses. The last time the three had been this way, the vegetation on the road had been far lower, worn down by the constant tramp of treasure hunters going back and forth from the town to the ruins and the Dungeons below. It seemed few people had used the road in the past month or two, though.

"It's the demons," Kellach said, as if he could read Driskoll's thoughts. "They've been getting bolder lately."

"As if our meeting with that thing—"

"Quasit."

"—whatever—this morning wasn't enough proof of that."

"It's not just us," Moyra said. "The Skinned Cat is lousy with frustrated fortune hunters these days. They're either too scared to follow their dreams and head out to the Dungeons of Doom, or they're mourning the friends they lost before they made it through the first level of the place."

"Our old friend the owlbear devastated the goblins there," Driskoll said. "You'd think that would make the place safer."

Kellach shook his head. "A dungeon's like any other environment: a delicate balance of creatures living off of one another in patterns built up over years or even centuries. Something happens to disrupt it like—well, like us setting the owlbear on an army of exposed goblins far from the safety of their home tunnels—and things change. And not always for the better."

"Don't try to make me feel bad about that," Driskoll said.

"Those goblins were ready to kill us." Driskoll shivered.

"The owlbear would have too," Moyra said. "If we'd given it half a chance."

"I'm not blaming anyone," said Kellach, "just explaining. When we get into the Dungeons, things are sure to have changed, maybe in ways that will be hard to predict. We have to be ready for just about anything."

"We need to get there, dive in, and find the Seal as quickly as we can," said Moyra.

"It may not be that simple."

"When has it ever been?" asked Driskoll with a wry smile.

The trio hiked the next couple miles in silence. Soon enough, Driskoll spotted the edge of the ruins of the once-great city that had stood almost next door to where Curston sat now.

"Does anyone know what happened here?" Driskoll asked, as they approached the vine-choked streets before them. It seemed like those same vines might, at any moment, pull down the tall fragments of crumbling walls from which they hung. Driskoll wondered if that might not be better for everyone—at least everyone in Curston.

"I don't," Kellach said. "Zendric might, but he's never talked about it. These ruins represent hundreds of years of decay. Curston—or Promise as it was known back then—was founded by the people who set up the original Seal as well as the Knights of the Silver Dragon, but who or what was here before that, I'm not sure."

"I hear tell that this was once the capital of an empire that ruled over the entire region," said Moyra. "One day, though, their sorcerer-king tore open a gate into the Abyss in an effort to cement his power. Unfortunately, all it earned him was an earlier death than the rest of the people who lived in the city."

"You can't believe everything you hear in the Skinned Cat," Kellach said.

"I'm sure Zendric's never been wrong either."

"Wait," Driskoll said, as they marched toward the tumbledown tower that had once housed the city's astronomical clock. "Do you hear that?"

The trio kept walking as they each cocked their ears and listened as hard as they could.

"Gods," Moyra said, disturbed. "I don't hear anything."

"Right," said Kellach. "No monsters growling, no henchmen cooking meals while they wait to see if their fortune-hunter bosses live or die."

"Not even a chirping bird," said Driskoll.

"What have we gotten ourselves into?" asked Moyra.

CHAPTER

15

The three fell silent again. Driskoll opened his mouth to speak a few times, but his reluctance to disturb the unnatural silence caused him to shut it every time. He wondered if this was some magic that affected everyone in the area or—worse yet—if they were all dead.

Soon they reached what had once been the central plaza in this ancient city. They picked their way through the ruined streets, cracked and overgrown, and past the buildings long since overtaken by the land around them. The remnants of countless camps of fortune hunters were strewn about the place. Such people were notorious for caring little about how they left the areas in which they did their "work." After all, if they fouled the lair of some horrible monsters, who would care?

"Oh, no," Moyra said, as they drew closer to the center of the square, where they knew a stairwell led down through the crumbling paving stones and into the Dungeons of Doom. She frowned, setting her jaw tight and resolute.

Driskoll started to ask what had upset Moyra. Then he spotted the first of the bodies.

A score of skeletons lay scattered about the square, most huddled together or brought down around the ashes of their campfires.

"No goblins did this," Driskoll said.

Moyra narrowed her eyes, which blazed with fury, at the entrance into the Dungeons of Doom. She looked like she might rip the head off of the next creature that had the gall to touch her. Driskoll made a mental note to make sure that wasn't him.

Kellach looked more serious than any time Driskoll could remember—since the day their mother had disappeared at least. At the time, Driskoll had only been seven years old, and Kellach but nine. Still, Kellach had refused to shed a single tear at the news that their mother was gone.

Driskoll, on the other hand, had wept for what seemed like weeks. He couldn't bring himself to believe his mother could truly be dead. She was a wizard, after all. How could someone so powerful be killed?

Kellach had pointed out the flaws in Driskoll's logic in painful detail, but Driskoll hadn't cared. He still looked for her every time he heard a light step enter their home—something that rarely happened these days.

Maybe that's why Driskoll had been so easily taken in

when Nahemah—a succubus—had shown up impersonating Jourdain. Having never given up hope, he had wanted to buy into the fantasy the demon tried to sell. Kellach hadn't, as he'd come to terms with Jourdain's death long ago.

Grim determination had gotten Kellach through that, the ability to believe in something with such clarity that it couldn't be untrue. Zendric had commented on it once to Driskoll while watching Kellach practice a simple spell.

"This is what makes it so hard for him to manage these 'easy' spells still. His mind is too strong to make matters so clearly false happen. When he matures, though, and can handle the most powerful spells, he will master them in no time at all. The strength of his will is what can make it so."

Right now, Driskoll wished they were all a bit older—a lot, even. As it was, they had barely three dozen years among them, less than a tenth of Zendric's age. If he couldn't stand up to Lexos, then what hope did they have?

"There it is," Kellach said, pointing at the stairs that led down through the plaza's floor into the hellish realm below. He went straight for it, picking his way over the bodies between him and his goal.

"Who do you think did this?" Driskoll said. Although he tried hard to stop it, he could hear his voice waver. He swallowed hard and tried again. "Killed all these people, I mean?"

"Does it matter?" Moyra said. Driskoll envied her steely voice. "We have to go into the Dungeons anyhow."

"Demons, maybe," Kellach said. "That would explain why everything's been burned. They favor fire."

"Do you think they got the owlbear too?" Driskoll asked. "Or the rest of the goblins? Or the . . . bugbear?"

Kellach grimaced as he reached the stairwell and stopped to look around them. Scorched bodies were sprawled about the place in every direction. "Anything that could do this wouldn't have a problem with owlbears or bugbears or goblins."

"Or us," Moyra said.

Driskoll shivered, but when Kellach and Moyra started down the stairwell, he followed right after them.

As they went down the steps, the walls of the stairwell cut off the lowering sun. The chill of the dungeons below seemed to seep through Driskoll's clothes and into his bones in mere moments. At least, he hoped that was what made him shiver so.

The three stopped at a rough landing at the bottom of the stairs to remove two lanterns from their packs. Moyra took one while Driskoll took the other. Kellach needed his hands free in case he had to cast a spell.

Driskoll filled his free hand with his sword. Moyra drew a long, sharp knife from a sheath on her belt. Kellach pulled a pouch full of ingredients for his spells from inside his robes and tied it to his own belt for easier access.

Driskoll looked up and saw the sign posted over the open doorway at the bottom of the stairs. It still said, "TURN BACK!"

but someone had scrawled something else across these words in a dark fluid that Driskoll tried to convince himself could not be blood.

"What does it say?" Moyra asked.

"Turn back." Driskoll smiled at her, and if her giggle at his joke sounded forced, neither of them wished to admit it.

"The other words," Moyra said. "The ones below that, silly."

"It's in Abyssal," Kellach said. "The language of demons."

"Zendric has you studying some pretty interesting things," said Moyra.

Driskoll didn't want to consider too closely the reasons why his brother might need to know the tongue in which demons conversed.

"It says, 'Too late!' " Kellach explained.

Driskoll grunted. "I didn't need to know that."

Kellach put his hand out, and Driskoll grabbed it. Moyra slapped hers on top of theirs.

"I just want—" Kellach started.

"Hold it," said Moyra. "If this is going to get all sloppy, I'm going to leave. Let's just get in there, do the job, and go home."

Driskoll stared at the girl. "But what if—"

Moyra winced. "What good does it do to go down that path? We know why we're here and what we have to do. That should be enough."

Kellach leaned over and kissed her on the cheek. While Moyra still stood stunned, Driskoll did the same for her other cheek.

"Fair enough," Kellach said, and he turned and plunged into the darkness beyond the doorway.

Inside, the walls and floor of the underground complex now known as the Dungeons of Doom were solid and smooth. The ceiling arced above them, coming to a point just out of even Kellach's reach. Fitted stones held everything together, even supplying buttresses at every intersection.

"What do you think these were originally built for?" Moyra asked. "These tunnels, I mean. It's not like the monsters just carved them out here under the old city like a bunch of giant termites, right?"

"Zendric once told me they had lots of uses: sewers, storage, whatever. Most important, though, they were to be the last line of defense against outside attacks. If invaders ever managed to breach the city walls, the people here would retreat to the complex below, where they could hold out for months or even years if they had to."

"That's ironic," said Driskoll. "Instead, they built tunnels that brought the demons to them."

The three walked in silence for a while then, the only sound was that of their shoes padding along the dungeon's stone floors. Driskoll noticed a disturbing lack of cobwebs throughout the place, but he didn't care to mention it. Instead, he watched Moyra lead them through the tunnels as best she could from her memories of the times they'd been down here before. Kellach followed close on her heels, while Driskoll brought up the rear, protecting their backs with his blade.

Soon, the passageway opened up into what had once been a large dining hall. Bits of rotted wood that had once been tables and chairs littered the place as far as the lanterns' lights would carry. The ceiling here was invisible in the blackness, far too high for Driskoll to see any hint of it. He looked back and saw old blood smeared on the wall behind them.

"I know where we are," he said. "This is where Durmok saved us from that zombie."

"That flaming-headed zombie," said Moyra, shuddering. She'd been the one down in the pit trap when the zombie had attacked, and she'd set its head on fire while trying to get away from it.

"Do you think you know where to go from here?" Kellach asked.

"I've never seen the Seal before. I don't know where it is." Frustration crept into her voice as she held her lantern aloft and peered into the edges of the darkness surrounding them.

"Are we just going to wander around here, hoping we can work our way deeper into the Dungeons until we stumble across this thing?" Driskoll asked. "Which we're not sure we'd know if we saw it?"

Kellach didn't answer for a moment. Then he said to Moyra, "Do you think you can find the goblin throne room?"

"I thought the owlbear chased most of the goblins out of here," said Driskoll, his voice trembling. He tried to clamp down on it but failed. "What good will that do us? Besides, the last time we saw the Goblin King, he ordered his warriors to kill us."

"Do you have to be such a coward?" Kellach said, glaring at his brother. "The goblins aren't there any more. If the owlbear didn't kill them all, then the treasure hunters or the demons probably got what was left."

"Kellach," Moyra said.

He ignored her and continued to lecture Driskoll. "Even if some of them survived, they likely ran off somewhere else. They'd have to be out of their minds to stick around here. You think we're crazy coming here? Try being three feet tall with orange skin."

"Kellach?" Moyra repeated.

Driskoll flushed in shame. He didn't want to be afraid of the goblins or of the other things that had to be roaming around the Dungeons in their place, but he couldn't help it. Kellach's know-it-all attitude only made things worse.

"The goblin throne room is at least somewhere for us to start," Kellach said. "And it's deeper into the Dungeons. It just makes—"

"Kellach!" Moyra shouted.

"What?" Kellach snapped back at Moyra.

"Shut your trap and look," she said softly, holding up her

lantern. The beam of light shot between the two brothers. They turned to gaze after it and saw a cluster of dim, low-slung lights reflecting back at them from the edges of the blackness.

For a moment Driskoll wondered what they might be. Then one of the lights blinked, and the other lights started to move forward. As they did, orange-colored faces emerged from the darkness.

"The goblins," Moyra said, "are here."

CHAPTER

16

A score or more of goblins surrounded them. Barely larger than the gnome Torin had rescued in the Town Hall that morning, their orange skin and sharp fangs marked them as something else. They wore strips of leather arranged off-kilter over simple rags that had gone from dirty to past filthy years ago. Most of them carried small, spiked clubs, but a few cocked back small bows fitted with tiny but dangerous arrows.

Stifling a scream, Driskoll spun toward the door behind them, hoping to flee, but a handful of larger creatures stood there clogging it. They stood twice as tall as the goblins, taller than Kellach and twice as broad as him too. Their fangs were longer, their eyes glowed an evil shade of green, and they wore chain mail shirts and carried heavy broadswords.

"Hobgoblins," Moyra said in the same tone she'd use if she'd found something nasty on the bottom of her boot.

" 'They're all gone,' " Driskoll said sarcastically. " 'They'd have to be crazy to hang around here.' "

"Shut up," Kellach said, irritation flashing in his voice. "It was a fine theory. Obviously I didn't have all the facts at hand."

"Obviously," Driskoll said. "Perhaps that's because you're not as smart as you—yikes!"

A slightly taller goblin scuttled out ahead of the others and stretched his arms in greeting. Something about the mad but brilliant light dancing in his eyes reminded Driskoll of someone.

The goblin said something in his guttural tongue, and the creatures surrounding the three Knights laughed low and loud.

"What did he say?" Moyra asked, her tone hushed. Neither she nor Driskoll spoke a lick of goblin, but Kellach had a good command of the language from his studies with Zendric.

"The Viceroy of the Hobgoblin Kingdom wishes to welcome us back to the Dungeons of Doom, and he hopes our stay will be a pleasant one, however short it may be."

"The Hobgoblin Kingdom?" Driskoll asked. "Since when have there been hobgoblins down here?"

Kellach spoke to the goblin in his own tongue. They chattered back and forth for a few minutes, talking like old friends. Driskoll and Moyra tried to interrupt a couple times, but Kellach waved them off.

"Just a bit more," he said once. "I think we're making progress."

119

Several minutes later, even the hobgoblins had started to get anxious. One of them even prodded the viceroy's back with the tip of his blade. At this, the viceroy turned around and launched into a blistering tirade. When the hobgoblins all pointed their swords at him, though, he put up his hands to apologize and then went back to talking with Kellach.

For a while, Driskoll shot mean looks at any of the goblins or hobgoblins who dared to look him in the eye. They usually met his stare for a few seconds but soon became bored and looked away. Eventually, Driskoll tired of this game too. His feet started to hurt, and he let the tip of his sword rest on the ground.

"Is this ever going to end?" Driskoll asked Moyra.

"It might," she said, cleaning her nails with the tip of her knife, ignoring the creatures surrounding them, who all kept a respectful distance away. "And then they might kill us—so I'm in no hurry."

"Good point," Driskoll said, staring once again at the weapons all around them.

"All right," Kellach said, turning away from the viceroy. "Good news. We're all set, I think."

"How's that?" Moyra said.

"We're going to let them take us to the goblin throne room—sorry, the hobgoblin throne room—so their new leader can decide what to do with us."

Moyra scowled at the viceroy and said to Kellach, "And this is good news?"

"It gets us one step closer to where we want to be—and with an armed guard, no less."

"But what will their leader want to do with us?" Driskoll said.

Kellach winced. "Well, the viceroy here tells me the Hobgoblin King likes his manflesh well done."

"And what did you say to that?" Driskoll said with a gasp.

"That we prefer to remain off the menu." Kellach paused for a second. "I got the biggest laugh from that."

The hobgoblins growled something at the viceroy, and he scampered over to Kellach and tugged on the edge of his robes.

"It's time to go," Kellach said. He and the others gathered their things and set off.

Driskoll kept his blade drawn, as did Moyra, mostly because no one had told him to put it away. The hobgoblins snorted at them with contempt, but the goblins all gave them plenty of space—especially Kellach.

"So what happened here?" Moyra asked.

"What do you mean?" said Kellach.

"You were talking with the viceroy there for a long time. You had to have learned more than where they wanted to take us."

Kellach smiled. "The viceroy here," he pointed to the goblin strutting next to him, having to trot at the same time to keep up, "used to be the Goblin King."

"I knew he looked familiar!" said Driskoll.

"It seems the owlbear nearly destroyed their fighting force

when we escaped from them. Less than a dozen of their best fighters survived."

"Ouch," said Driskoll.

"Don't feel too bad for them," Moyra said. "Remember, they'd just ordered our deaths."

Driskoll knew that was one day he'd never forget. Still, to realize that he and his friends had caused the deaths of dozens of goblins sobered him. Sometimes their adventures seemed like something out of a book, a story in which they starred, which meant that nothing bad could ever happen to them.

As Driskoll marched deeper into the Dungeons of Doom, he realized that he, Kellach, and Moyra had once again found themselves in a situation that could prove to be the death of them. And if it didn't, many others might die instead. These thoughts terrified him so much that he jumped when Moyra put a hand on his shoulder.

"Are you all right?" she asked. He saw true concern in her eyes.

"Just a little nervous, I guess," he said. "It's not every day I get hauled before royalty to justify my actions on pain of death."

"The Hobgoblin King's not really royalty," Kellach said, missing entirely how bothered Driskoll was. "He's more like a bully that burst in and set himself up as boss.

"After the goblins lost most of their fighting strength, this band of hobgoblins that lived nearby found out about it. They came in and killed a few more goblins to prove their superiority, and then put themselves in charge of the place. They had a couple dozen goblin fighters they'd enslaved from another tribe, lower in the Dungeons, and they set them up over these goblins as their enforcers."

"So there aren't many hobgoblins?" Driskoll asked.

"You're watching the backs of most of them," Kellach said, pointing at the hobgoblins ahead of them. "The others serve in the Hobgoblin King's court. They don't leave much. They have the goblins to do most of their dirty work for them."

"So the ones with us drew the short straw?" said Moyra.

"No," said Kellach. "They just like to kill things."

The trio walked in silence for a while, letting the goblins and hobgoblins lead them on a twisting path to the territory they'd managed to carve out for themselves in the Dungeons of Doom. Driskoll watched the nearest creatures, studying them as best he could, hoping to learn something that could help them later. The few times one of the goblins returned his gaze, they glanced at him with trembling eyes and then looked away.

"Do we have a plan here?" Driskoll said, a feeling of dread creeping into his belly. "Other than 'let the monsters eat us,' of course."

"Of course," said Kellach.

"Do you mind sharing it with us?"

Kellach paused. "It's not really that firm yet."

"I'd get to work on that," Moyra said, a hint of urgency in

her voice. "I'm starting to recognize some of these passages. We're getting closer by the minute.

"You can't rush a good idea," Kellach said, calm as ever. "Don't worry. It will all come together."

Driskoll fell into a sullen silence. Kellach seemed to always be doing things like this. He got himself into trouble after trouble and had absolute faith that his wits would get him out of it. The worst part was he usually dragged Driskoll and Moyra into the trouble with him.

"I think you're enjoying this," Moyra said to Kellach.

"Heading into the goblin throne room deep in the Dungeons of Doom on a mission to foil a plot that could destroy every living soul in our hometown, including our families and every friend we've ever had?" Kellach grinned. "You bet I'm loving it."

"Well, I hope you've firmed up that plan of yours," Moyra said as they marched into an open room that faced a tall pair of ironbound doors. "We're here."

CHAPTER

17

A rmored goblins bearing long spears stood to either side of the entrance, and others scrambled forward to pull the doors open. Somewhere beyond the doors, poorly tuned horns trumpeted the arrival of guests to the kingdom. The great slabs of banded wood creaked back on rusted hinges, slowly revealing the cavernous hall beyond.

The hobgoblins led the way into the hall, just as they had during the entire march there. The goblins surrounding the three kids edged farther away from them, giving them room to keep their clubs up and ready to swing. The viceroy walked alongside Kellach, just as before.

To Driskoll, it seemed that the viceroy meant to show his support for Kellach, but he couldn't imagine why. If the Hobgoblin King was as bad as he'd heard, Driskoll suspected the viceroy courted death to associate so openly with human intruders. Perhaps he still felt grateful for when the three of them had saved him from being trapped in the spiritkeeper so many months ago.

Of course, that hadn't stopped him from ordering their deaths.

Driskoll gaped at the vast hall as they entered it. It looked much like he remembered it, only dirtier and in worse shape. While the goblins hadn't been able to maintain the place as well as the dwarfs who had likely built it, the hobgoblins had actively gone about tearing the place apart.

Graffiti covered the walls as high as ten feet up, making the pillars that held up the high ceiling seem like the legs of giants with dirty feet. The scrawls depicted all manner of horrible things. In one scene, a hobgoblin wearing a crown battled a winged, horned demon with a curving, spiked tail. In another, a snakelike demon squeezed to death a handful of goblins caught in its coils.

The red carpet that ran the length of the hall had been torn and smelled of urine. Large chunks had been chipped from the stone throne. Its bed-sized seat cushion no longer sat there. A nest made of what looked like bits of the carpet and other unidentifiable things—bones, perhaps—sat in its place.

The whole place reeked. Driskoll's eyes watered as they approached the throne and the massive, orange-skinned creature that sat upon it, wallowing in his nasty nest. He wanted to plug his nose, but that would have meant setting down either his lantern or his sword. As he wasn't yet willing to give up either, he suffered through it instead, hoping the stench would soon overload his sense of smell and leave him mercifully unable to smell a thing.

The Hobgoblin King laughed long and loud as the procession led the Knights closer to his dais. He towered over even the other hobgoblins standing guard next to him, although he looked like an athlete long since gone to seed. His huge, naked belly hung out over his tattered excuse for a kilt, which looked like it hadn't seen a washboard since before Driskoll had been born. Atop his head, he wore a golden crown three sizes too small for him. In other circumstances, Driskoll might have laughed at it, but he couldn't find anything funny about it right now.

The Hobgoblin King glared down at the three kids from his stolen throne and snarled something at the viceroy. Spittle flew from his cheeks, which bulged with the remnants of some long-ago meal upon which he still chewed. When he finished, he sat back in the throne, reclining in the mess of a nest, and picked his long, vicious teeth with the sharp end of a shattered bone.

"He wants to know why the viceroy dared to bring him a meal without slaughtering it first," said Kellach.

Driskoll gasped and instantly regretted it, since he sucked a great gulp of the foul air into his lungs as he did. This set him into a coughing fit that lasted until Moyra stepped over and slapped him several times on the back. In the meantime, all conversation stopped, and even the Hobgoblin King stared down at Driskoll with a mixed look of surprise and disgust.

"I'm okay," Driskoll said, wiping the tears from his eyes once he could breathe again. "Tell them to go ahead with their plans to devour us."

Kellach nodded to the viceroy, who bowed his head to the Hobgoblin King until his ears scraped the tattered carpet. Then he stood back up, tall and proud, and spoke directly to the tyrant sitting in his seat.

Kellach translated for the other two kids: "The viceroy explains that we are the heroes from the upper world who once destroyed his kingdom. Without our efforts, the goblins would never have been so weak that the hobgoblins would have dared to attack them. He brought us here so that the king could thank us personally for playing such a substantial part in his good fortune."

The Hobgoblin King's eyes grew wide at first, possibly in fear. As the viceroy continued speaking, though, that fear shifted to irritation and then anger.

"He doesn't seem all that grateful," Moyra said.

The Hobgoblin King let loose a howl that seemed to shake the buttresses holding up the ceiling of the hall. A few shards of stone tumbled down from the ceiling, leading Driskoll to glance up to where a window had once channeled bright sunlight into the hall through a cunning system of mirrors. Now, though, something blocked the light. A score of smoky braziers flickered along the walls and next to the throne, instead, casting everything in a hellish light. Driskoll couldn't tell what it was the goblins burned in those wide, shallow bowls, but it didn't smell anything like wood.

Kellach grimaced. "While the king seems to respect our legendary prowess, he doesn't care for the attitude our arrival seems to have given his viceroy."

The viceroy started to respond, but another earsplitting howl from the Hobgoblin King cut him off. The viceroy stepped back, closer to Kellach. Kellach reached out and put a hand on the small creature's shoulder, as a mother would do to protect a child.

The king scowled, and when the viceroy opened his mouth, the king snarled him down. Perched on his heels now, atop the edge of the seat of the throne, the king rubbed his rough-whiskered chin as he considered the three humans in his midst and what their fate might be.

Soon, the king frowned, but he seemed to have come to a resolution in his mind. He pointed at the viceroy and grunted something at him. Then he reached toward the three humans and clenched his fists. He gabbed at them in his strange, harsh tongue.

Kellach's face fell.

"What is it?" Driskoll said. He looked down at his skinny arms and legs and wondered how anyone could think they could make a proper meal of him.

"For what we have done to the goblins—and for what we might do to his kingdom if pressed—the king has decided our fate." Kellach put his face into his hands for a moment. When he removed them, he looked pale and disturbed. "He's decided to set us free."

Driskoll let loose with a long and happy whoop, and Moyra joined in right beside him. The two hugged each other and tried to sweep Kellach into their embrace. He would have nothing to do with it, though. Instead, he stood there, stone still, and glared at the Hobgoblin King.

The viceroy shrugged his shoulders and reached up to turn Kellach around toward the exit. Instead, Kellach pushed the goblin away and snarled something at the Hobgoblin King.

Driskoll had never seen his brother look so evil. He seemed prepared to launch himself over the heads of all the creatures between him and the throne and beat the Hobgoblin King to death with his tiny crown.

"What are you saying to him?" Moyra asked, frozen in Driskoll's arms.

Driskoll pulled himself free and grabbed his brother from behind, spinning him. "That better be goblin for 'Thank you, and good-bye.' "

"You're going to have to trust me," Kellach said, his voice calm and steady. Driskoll knew his brother well enough, though, to see that underneath it all he was scared. Worse yet, there was something Kellach wasn't telling him.

"Kellach—" he started.

"Hey," Kellach said, looking deep into Driskoll's eyes,

"would I do something that could get us killed?"

"Yes," Moyra said, "and I can give examples."

Kellach took one of his hands off Driskoll and put it on Moyra's shoulder instead. "You're going to have to trust me," he said again.

Driskoll sighed. "We don't have any choice." He looked at Moyra. "He's the only one who can speak goblin."

Moyra slapped her hands over her face. "All right," she said. "Just get it over with. If I'm going to die, make it quick, though, would you? I can't take the suspense."

The Hobgoblin King snarled out an order of some sort, and the hobgoblin warriors closed in from all sides, pressing their goblin allies in next to their prey. The hobgoblins leveled their blades at the trio, paying special attention to Kellach. The viceroy clung to Kellach's leg, and Driskoll thought the little creature might start to weep.

"So what's the story?" Driskoll said to his brother. The two boys and Moyra stood pressed together, their backs to one another, as they looked outward to face the hobgoblins threatening them.

"It's all going to plan," Kellach said with a satisfied smile. "We've been sentenced to death."

CHAPTER

18

The goblins around Driskoll, Moyra, and Kellach started to shiver. As they shuddered against one another, their movement picked up momentum. They shook harder and harder and started to wail in time with their shakes.

The wailing started soft, almost an involuntary, mass moan, but it fast built into a tuneless tone of horror that grew louder and louder. Driskoll reached up and covered his ears to shut out the worst of it, but it kept growing worse and worse until he wondered if they'd been sentenced to die by the lethal whining of a gaggle of goblins.

A savage roar from the Hobgoblin King cut off the noise, and each of the goblins shut his mouth. They continued to tremble, though, and Driskoll worried that the awful noise might erupt from them again at any moment.

The hobgoblins who had been guarding them herded the goblins around the humans. They used their swords to form a protective layer of the littler creatures around the three Knights. Then, at a signal from a hobgoblin near the rear, they all turned for the exit and started out of the hall.

As they approached the high doors, Driskoll's ears echoed with the sound of the Hobgoblin King's belly-jiggling laugh. When the group finally managed to clear the hall, the doors screeched shut behind them and cut the king's cackling off.

"Explain to me now," Moyra said, gripping her knife as she looked back over her shoulder at Kellach, "why this is a good thing."

Driskoll wondered if she meant to use the knife on his brother or the creatures around them. As he adjusted his grasp on his own sword, he searched his own heart for an answer to the same question.

"We need to get to the Seal, right? This is the fastest way."

Driskoll groaned, unable to keep quiet any longer. "Is the afterlife on the other side of the Seal? They kill us, and we end up right there?"

Kellach smiled, despite his brother's distress. "Close," he said, "but not quite."

"If we get out of this, I think I'm going to kill you," Moyra said. "Then we can test Driskoll's theory for sure."

Kellach raised his eyebrows at Moyra, who glared back at him for a full minute. Finally, she gave up, letting her shoulders sag. "Fine," she said. "Just, when you explain it, try not to make it worse than it already seems."

"I'll try."

The hobgoblins turned the entire procession to the left and started down a series of halls and passages that Driskoll had never seen before.

"The goblins, hobgoblins, and every other creature in the Dungeons of Doom have lived in the shadow of the Great Seal for centuries. We think we have it bad in Curston because we have to deal with the occasional monster that manages to slip past the Seal and make its way through the wilderness to our walled city.

"Imagine living right on top of it instead. Lots of the monsters that escape from the Abyss never bother to leave the Dungeons. They find plenty of prey right here. If they don't get their fill of the creatures who make their homes here, they can always feast on the parties of treasure hunters that regularly make their way here in search of fortune and glory."

"You're saying we should feel sorry for the creatures that just condemned us to death." Moyra shook her head and sighed.

"To be fair, I essentially asked for that, although I had to insult the Hobgoblin King to make it happen. I didn't think he'd go along with it if I put in a polite request. He's a suspicious sort."

"Forgive me if I'm slow," said Driskoll, "but why did you do that, again?"

Kellach smiled, and Driskoll had to fight the urge to smash him with the pommel of his sword.

"Remember this morning at the meeting when Zendric said the Seal was like a rotten cork?"

Driskoll nodded. "Things are leaking out around it."

"More and more all the time. The things that live down here have been taking the brunt of that. It seems that the hobgoblins' old lair was deep in the Dungeons, closer to where the Seal sits.

"When the Seal started to give way, the hobgoblins tried lots of different things to get it to stop. Some of them gave up and headed for higher ground. That's how the Hobgoblin King came to take over the Goblin King's realm.

"Others, though, decided to try something different. For as long as they've lived near the Seal and had to deal with that, they didn't really understand what it is. Mostly, they still don't. They just want it to stay shut and for the demons behind it to leave them alone.

"So, they started to pray to it."

Kellach stopped for a moment to let that sink in.

"Gods," said Moyra. "You mean they worship it?"

Kellach nodded.

"They took a half-stuffed hole to the Abyss and turned it into a god?" Driskoll stared at the creatures around them, seeing them in a new, darker light.

"Effectively, yes," Kellach said. "Unlike with most followers, though, they only wanted one thing from it: to stay shut; to keep the monsters away. After a while, though, it was clear that prayers wouldn't be enough. So they started to present it with offerings."

Driskoll tried to swallow, but his mouth had run dry. He could tell he didn't like where this was headed.

"What kind of offerings?" he rasped.

"Food, weapons, wine—the usual things—at first. Some of these worked for a while. The demons enjoyed the food and the wine, but they had little use for the rest. Soon, they craved more, though, and ignored the offerings. In fact, because they now knew someone lived nearby, their incursions became more frequent instead of less.

"Then one of the hobgoblin leaders had a brilliant idea. They had captured a group of treasure hunters and needed to decide what to do with them."

Driskoll felt his stomach flip over. He'd been right. He didn't want to hear this.

"They took the prisoners down to the Seal and staked them out there in front of it. Then they ran away. When they came back the next day to investigate, there wasn't much left of the prisoners, but there weren't any demons around either.

"Since then, the hobgoblins have been making regular sacrifices to the demons."

Driskoll threw up on the goblin in front of him. The creature squealed in terror and then disgust. He stampeded over three goblins and a hobgoblin in front of him in his desperate attempt to flee. As he skipped past the hobgoblin, though, the larger creature reached out and grabbed him by his neck.

The hobgoblin hoisted the slimy, smelly goblin up to eye level and growled into the terrified creature's face as he tried to free himself. The goblin's eyes grew wide and his efforts became wilder as he realized the hobgoblin meant to strangle him.

The other hobgoblins chortled in delight as they watched the hapless goblin struggle. The poor creature's strength began to flag, and his kicking legs started to slow. The goblins watching this scene cowered in fear.

"Put him down!" Moyra said. She punctuated her command with a stab of her knife. When the hobgoblin ignored her, she tickled his ribs with it. That got his attention.

The hobgoblin hurled the half-strangled goblin aside and spun to face Moyra. She shoved the edge of her knife up against his throat and spat in his eyes. "Do that again, and I'll carve you a new smile!" she whispered.

The passageway had become so quiet that her words echoed down it undeterred.

The hobgoblin started to bring up his sword, but Driskoll leaped forward and slapped it down with his own blade. Moyra pressed her knife into the hobgoblin's orange flesh until a trickle of fire-colored blood ran down its edge.

The viceroy jumped up and snarled something at the hob-goblin. The larger creature, taken by surprise, stepped back and lowered his sword. He stared at the viceroy for a moment, unsure how to deal with this new show of spine in the former Goblin King.

Then Kellach said something to the hobgoblin. The hobgoblin stepped back, grunting. He spat a few words back at Kellach and turned to lead the group down the passageway again.

Moyra wanted to stop and see how the goblin she'd tried to save had fared. The viceroy grabbed her hand and pulled her along instead.

"What's the idea?" she said. "He needs help."

"The viceroy has a new name for that one, now that he doesn't have to go to the Chamber of the Great Seal with us," said Kellach.

"Oh yeah?" Moyra asked. "What's that?"

"Lucky."

CHAPTER

19

After what seemed like hours, the group wound its way into a large chamber. A while back, the smooth-cut halls had given way to rough-hewn tunnels and then to natural formations connected by a few handmade passages. Water dripped from the walls and ceiling in some places and made the floors slick.

As the way grew rougher, the goblins and hobgoblins became more nervous. By the time they reached the cavern, their legs shook with every step. It amazed Driskoll that they could go on at all.

The upper portions of the Dungeons had been pitch black. Driskoll and Moyra still carried their lanterns, and a number of the goblins lit the way with guttering torches too.

As Driskoll entered this cavern with the others arranged all around him, though, the first thing he noticed was that it was lit from within. The floor of the place lay flat and level, clearly made that way by skilled stonecutters, but the walls remained unfinished. At the far end of the hall, a tall, wide tunnel started but terminated in a wall made of something that glowed like the embers of a dying fire.

"This is the Chamber of the Great Seal," Kellach said.

As the words left his brother's lips, Driskoll saw dozens of odd-shaped rock formations where the dead-end tunnel began. As the group pushed farther into the cavern, though, he realized these rocks weren't rocks at all, but bones.

The bones had been stripped clean of flesh and blackened in some horrible fire, which made them seem like the opposite of the sun-bleached skeleton that hung in the window of an alchemy shop back in Curston.

In the center of the skeletons lay four sets of manacles chained to iron anchors set in the cavern floor. Dark stains covered these and the space around them, and there were scratches on the nearest wall.

The hobgoblin leading the execution crew paused once everyone had made it into the cavern. He looked back and counted heads to make sure that no one had tried to slip out of their duties at the last second. Then, with a serious grunt, he pulled them behind him.

Driskoll peered into the tunnel, at the strange wall that ended it. The material there seemed like a sheet of ice that had started to crack in the warm air of the coming spring. The solid stuff—the bits that didn't glow—looked like a great shield made of tarnished silver and engraved with a circle of protection that spanned from side to side.

The circle bore many cracks in its edges, though, which Driskoll knew made it next to useless. He hadn't studied magic like his brother, but he'd picked up a bit during all those long afternoons in Zendric's tower, waiting for Kellach's lessons to be over. The fact that the Seal—for that is what this had to be—still held back anything at all was a testament to the incredible magic that had forged it in the first place.

The light in the cavern came from between the cracks in the Seal. These glowed with a fiery light that shed enough heat that Driskoll couldn't see why the metal parts of the Seal didn't glow from it too.

He could see a dragon design in the center of the Seal. This part, at least, looked solid and unbreakable. Not a single crack appeared in it, although they radiated out from its every edge.

"So," Moyra said to Kellach, "what's the next part of the plan?"

Kellach grimaced, never taking his gaze from the glowing Seal. "That's the part that's not so firm yet."

"I'd say the deadline for that is here," said Driskoll.

"We have one thing in our favor," Kellach said. "Lexos hasn't made it here yet."

The lead hobgoblin ordered a few of the goblins forward and pointed at the manacles on the floor. The goblins set about removing the remains still stuck in two of the sets of manacles and clearing the area of the other bits and pieces lying around.

"If he doesn't show up here soon, we may have other problems," said Moyra.

The viceroy peered up at Kellach and spoke a few words that could only have been a plea for action. Kellach reached down and patted the goblin leader on the head.

"Get ready," Kellach said just loud enough for Driskoll and Moyra to hear. "We make our move when I say the word."

"Is there a plan?" Driskoll asked.

"Stop them before they kill us."

Moyra grinned. "I like that plan," she said. "Simple and to the point. I could live by words like those."

"Or die by them," Torin said, as he strode into the room.

CHAPTER

20

Driskoll jumped up and yelled, "Dad!"

Torin stood in the entrance to the cavern, dressed in his watcher's uniform, his sword held out before him at the ready. Lochinvar sat perched on his shoulder, his wings stretched wide.

The goblins froze and stared at the watcher in terror. The look of fury on Torin's face would have been enough to cause them to give themselves all up, Driskoll knew, if not for the presence of the hobgoblins keeping them in line.

The hobgoblin leader pointed his broadsword at Torin and unleashed a battle cry that would have caused lesser men to turn and flee. The captain of the watch of Curston, however, barked out a bitter laugh.

The hobgoblins came at him with their blades drawn.

"Scatter!" Torin shouted, as he launched himself at the creatures surrounding his sons and their friend.

Kellach hurled himself to the left, gathering up the viceroy in his arms as he went. Lochinvar dove off of Torin's shoulder, scudded along the cavern floor, and pulled up to land on his master's outstretched arm. Moyra went to the right, pulling Driskoll along behind her. He didn't protest. He was too busy drawing his sword and looking to see which hobgoblin might come at them first.

Moyra drew her knife with her left hand and tossed it into her right as she let Driskoll go. The two of them looked at each other and then Torin, who stood staring about the cavern, sizing the situation up. He gave no sign that he noticed them or Kellach, who had started to chant something, but Driskoll knew that his father's sharp eyes hadn't missed a thing, them included.

A flash erupted from Kellach's direction, and the goblins and hobgoblins flinched at the searing burst of light.

Moyra and Driskoll knew this was their signal to act. They launched themselves toward the goblins, waving their blades as they roared at the top of their lungs. It terrified Driskoll to run toward the creatures, but he knew he had no other choice. It was time to fight or be slaughtered.

The goblins sprinted away from them, and Driskoll's heart leaped. Several of the creatures stumbled into one another or froze up as they tried to decide how best to avoid all four of the tall, pasty-skinned intruders and their hobgoblin commanders too. Most of them abandoned their weapons, although a few clung to them as a child might to a favorite doll for moral support.

The hobgoblins, in stark contrast, stood ready to use their broadswords. They outnumbered Torin, Kellach, Moyra, and Driskoll two to one, but Torin's surprise appearance had unnerved them.

Torin charged through the center of the chamber, dashing straight for the leader who had howled so horribly at him. The hobgoblin met the watcher's attack, snarling at Torin as their blades clashed.

While the hobgoblin might have been the more ferocious fighter, he had nothing on Torin's skill. The watcher countered the hobgoblin's clumsy attack and then slashed at his sword arm, slicing through the orange skin there.

The creature snarled as he dropped his weapon. He held his wound tight and waited for the deathblow to follow.

Torin brought the point of his sword to his foe's throat and held it there. It would only take a flick of Torin's wrist to slay the creature and allow the watcher to move on to rest of the creatures, killing as many as he must to save the lives of his children and their friend.

Everyone else in the room—including the other hobgoblins—froze and waited to see what would happen. Driskoll held his own sword at the ready as he and Moyra pulled up short of the cavern's exit. Driskoll had pulled her back as they reached the portal, not wanting to get drawn into the caverns beyond and perhaps get trapped between the goblins and hobgoblins. He knew they all had to stay together.

The terrified goblins huddled against the wall to the left of the chamber's exit. In their terror, they'd taken a wrong turn and been pressed into a niche there. Cornered, they turned to watch their hobgoblin masters fight the pink-skinned invaders.

Torin nicked the hobgoblin across the throat with his sword, then turned and stepped aside, keeping his sword trained on his foe every instant. With his free hand, he pointed toward the exit.

The hobgoblin snarled at the watcher. He glanced at the open passageway with slitted eyes, sizing up his chances. Before he could make a dash for freedom, though, the watcher brought his blade up to his throat again.

"Kellach," Torin said. "I want you to tell this bully something for me."

"All right, Dad," Kellach said, his voice uncertain.

"I don't want to kill them—I don't have the time—but I will if they force me to. Every one of them."

Kellach spoke to the hobgoblin leader without hesitation. He spoke loud and clear, making sure that everyone in the cavern could hear his every word.

"I ask him only to leave us here alone in the Chamber of the Great Seal. He can then let the Seal do with us as it wishes."

Kellach kept translating. Driskoll watched the faces of the hobgoblins around them, measuring their reactions to his father's words. He found it impossible to read their monstrous faces.

"They will have appeased their Seal-god," Torin said. "They will have fulfilled their orders. And they will get to live."

A number of the hobgoblins nodded at this wisdom. Their leader stared at Torin, who pulled his sword back once more and jerked his head at the exit.

Driskoll held his breath.

CHAPTER

21

The hobgoblin leader dashed toward the entrance, scooping up his broadsword as he went. The others didn't even take time to glance backward before following him out.

Once the creatures had left, Torin turned toward Moyra and his sons, his blade still out, his eyes still burning with fury. "I ought to chain the three of you to the top of the obelisk in the Great Circle. You promised me you would stay home—"

"We never 'promised' anything," Kellach cut in. "I said 'We'll listen.' We listened to what you said—and then we did what had to be done."

Torin stormed over to Kellach. "You think you're clever, son, and you are. Perhaps too clever for your own good. You knew what I meant. I told you stay put, and you left the house. You disobeyed me."

Kellach started to say something, then clamped his mouth shut and stared up at his father. Although Kellach had grown a lot over the past year, Torin still towered over him and had an easy fifty pounds on him, all of it muscle. The captain of the watch intimidated people as part of his job. When he turned that skill on his sons, it was no less effective.

Getting no response, Torin continued, "You are a brilliant boy, Kellach, but you're just a boy. You haven't the years to have any real wisdom. I knew this would happen. That's why I ordered you to stay home." Torin shook his head and then growled into his son's face. "Why is it that you never listen?"

Kellach's face grew redder and redder as his father spoke, but he didn't say a word. Driskoll knew that if something didn't happen soon his brother would either dissolve or explode, and he didn't want to watch either thing happen. To stop his father meant standing up to him, though, and he wasn't sure he was up to that any more than it seemed Kellach might be.

"We were trying to save Curston," Moyra said, stomping up to stand next to Kellach. Driskoll followed after her, although not so eagerly.

Torin turned on Moyra. "That's not your job. It's mine."

"Well, if you'd been doing it—"

"How did you find us?" Driskoll asked, hoping to distract his father and prevent this fight. It had been brewing for a long time, but this wasn't the time or place to have it.

"I woke up in the cathedral, and Latislav told me you'd just left. I ran home, but you'd already gone." Torin stabbed a finger at Lochinvar. Perched on Kellach's shoulder, the dragonet seemed to be trying to hide behind his master's head. "Fortunately, your little friend here had a good idea where you'd gone. He led me right to you."

"Kel-lach safe," Locky said.

Before Torin or Kellach could start in on each other again, Driskoll saw someone tug on Kellach's sleeve. He looked down and saw the viceroy staring up at them. He said something serious to Kellach and then shook his hand. Seeing the tiny orange paw in his brother's hand almost made Driskoll laugh. He looked around, though, and saw all of the other goblins staring up at them with respect in their eyes, and that quieted the urge.

The goblins turned and raced out of the chamber, each of them following in the viceroy's footsteps. As they filed out, Driskoll wondered whether he'd ever see any of them again—especially the viceroy—or if the hobgoblins would kill them out of shame or sheer spite. Somehow, despite his natural revulsion of them, he'd come to see them more as people than creatures, and he hoped they'd survive.

"Now," Torin said, his mood still black, "why in all the gods' names shouldn't I toss you all into jail when I get you back home?"

"It's Lexos, Dad. He's after the Key of Order," Kellach said.

"I know that. That's why I went to talk with Latislav, to get the piece of it hidden in the cathedral. Breddo told me that Lexos had his hands on the first one."

"He did?" Moyra couldn't suppress her pride in her father for doing such a thing, but she then scowled at Torin. "And did you arrest him for his efforts?"

"He's too smart to be caught that easily."

"But you apparently are not, old friend."

A shiver shot up Driskoll's spine at the sound of that voice.

Driskoll's eyes locked on Kellach's. He could see that his brother had recognized the voice too. Both of them froze.

CHAPTER

22

D ad!" Driskoll shouted. "Dad, it's—"

The red-robed cleric sauntered into the chamber, a smug smirk playing on his lips.

"Lexos." The name left Driskoll as a whisper.

Lexos chuckled. "You children have caused me nothing but trouble—until today."

As Lexos spoke, he reached into his pocket and pulled out a short length of rope that writhed like a snake in his grasp. He reached down and pulled Torin's hands together with his other hand. Then the rope zipped around Torin's wrists, binding them tight.

Kellach let loose with a spell, but Lexos sloughed it off with a wave of his hand.

"You're a fool, boy, if you think such useless cantrips can harm me. I would have thought that Zendric would have taught you more respect for your betters. I know your mother would have."

At the mention of his mother, Driskoll started forward. Before he took a full step, though, Kellach reached out and pulled him back. He drew Driskoll closer to him with a trembling arm.

Lexos laughed at Driskoll and his sword. "Do you think I'd let you hurt me with your pathetic blade? Your brother has the right of it, finally. He knows I could kill the lot of you with but a single word from my lips."

The cleric curled his lips in an evil smile. "And perhaps I still will."

Lexos knelt down next to Torin and started going through his pockets. As he did, the smile melted from his face and became a frustrated frown. He began to pat down every inch of the watcher's uniform, getting more agitated as he went.

"Where is it?" he said. "Where is it?"

When no one answered him, Lexos stood up and shoved the frozen Torin over with a solid boot in his back. Moyra kicked back her arm, holding her dagger by its point, but Kellach grabbed its handle before she could throw it. She glared up at him, but he ignored her.

"Come, Kellach," Lexos said. "Don't tell me you don't know where it is, clever one. How unlike you that would be."

Kellach just spat on the ground between himself and the cleric. For a moment, Driskoll wondered if Kellach really did know where the third part of the Key was and just hadn't chosen to reveal it yet. When he saw his brother's face flush with anger, though—the same sort of frustration he'd shown when Lexos had gotten away from them at Zendric's tower—he knew that Kellach didn't have a clue.

"Predictable," Lexos sneered at Kellach. "You share both Zendric's ambitions and his arrogance. When I realized Torin didn't have the key, it was all too easy to trick you into coming here. With him hurt and me missing, you'd assume I'd gathered the pieces of the Key. There would only be one way to stop me, right?"

Driskoll and Moyra gasped. A gurgle escaped from Kellach's throat.

"Of course the new Knights raced headlong off to the Dungeons of Doom at the first threat of danger to their hometown. And of course Torin chased after you as soon as he learned what you'd done. And I knew that one of you would bring the last part of the key with him. Right. To. Me."

Kellach glared at Lexos but said not a word. Driskoll didn't understand this strange change in his brother's demeanor. He'd expected Kellach to produce the Key or announce some intricate plan in which he'd anticipated Lexos's every move and already remade the Seal while Lexos was talking. But all Kellach did was turn even redder and lower his head.

Lexos stared down at Torin for a moment, then spat on his frozen form. "Pathetic." He glared at Driskoll, then Kellach. "Like father, like sons. All too ready to sacrifice yourselves for the good of others."

Lexos sniggered. "Let's see if we can help you take care of that ambition at least.

"Where is it?" Lexos hissed down at Torin.

The captain of the watch blinked his eyes for a moment. He started to move and then realized his hands were bound behind him. When he rolled over onto his back, Lexos glared down at him.

"Where is it?" he said.

Torin growled, then said, "What makes you think I'd bring it with me?"

"Perhaps on the off chance you'd have to bargain for your children's lives."

Torin had long mastered the unreadable face. His fellow watchers refused to play cards with him any longer.

Lexos, though, had other ways of learning the truth. He spat out a blasphemous prayer to his dark god, and a reddish glow enveloped his head and then disappeared into his ears as if sucked into them through a straw.

Driskoll charged at Lexos, hauling his blade over his head in a two-handed grip. Moyra came right behind him, slinging her dagger. Kellach shouted a few words Driskoll couldn't understand, and a light shot forth from his hands and burst right in front of Lexos's eyes.

The cleric staggered backward, blinking and cursing. As he moved, he made a strange gesture and then said something horrible.

Driskoll didn't understand Lexos's words, but he didn't want to. Despite his ignorance, the phrases slammed into his brain and twisted about in his head until only one thing could escape: fear.

Instead of slashing down through the cleric's robes and flesh with his blade, Driskoll turned away from him, nearly tripping over his own feet as he fled. No conscious thought made him do this. He had no such thoughts to spare. The only thing he could think of was to get away from Lexos as fast as he could.

Driskoll dashed down the dead-end tunnel and came smack up against the Great Seal itself. While being this close to the crumbling circle of protection would normally have sent him racing in the other direction, all Driskoll could manage to do was stop there in front of it—the heat radiating from it searing his skin—and curl up into a ball.

Someone grabbed Driskoll as he went trembling to the floor, and he screamed. The grabber screamed back, and then someone else grabbed them both, which sent all three of them wailing. A long, horrible moment passed before Driskoll had to stop to catch his breath. He realized then that Kellach and Moyra were the ones huddled on the floor next to him.

"Leave them alone!" Torin growled. Peeking out between his fingers, Driskoll saw his father struggling to stand, but a quick kick from Lexos sent him back to the floor again.

CHAPTER

23

Lexos stood over Torin and laughed. "So these are the new Knights of the Silver Dragon?" he said, shaking his head. "Our fabled order has fallen on harder times than I'd thought."

"They're children," Torin said. "Let them go."

Driskoll had seen the look in Torin's eyes before. If the watcher could have freed his hands at that moment, Lexos would have been dead before he could see the man move. Struggle as he could, though, Torin could not make the magical bonds give.

"The point isn't that they're children," Lexos said. "I have no interest in children." He leaned over and hissed at the captain of the watch, "It's that they're your children. Yours and Jourdain's and Breddo's. But most vitally at the moment, yours."

Lexos reached into the folds of his robe and produced two parts of the Key of Order, the bits that looked like the body and the head of a silver dragon. He fitted the two together.

"I have two parts of the Key," the cleric said. "I mean to have the third. You will give it to me."

"I don't have it," Torin said between gritted teeth.

Surprise flashed across Lexos's face. The spell he'd cast earlier, Driskoll knew, allowed him to detect any lies. Torin, it seemed, had given Lexos something he hadn't expected: the truth.

"How could you not bring it?" Lexos said, astonished, rolling his tongue around in his mouth. "You knew I didn't have it. You must have guessed that the reason I attacked you in that cursed cathedral was to plant the idea in the heads of your sons that I had it. You knew as well as I did that they'd race here to try to stop me."

Lexos leaned over Torin and ground his knee into the watcher's back. As Torin squirmed in pain, Lexos rasped at him, "It was the only thing you could have brought with you to bargain for their lives."

"I don't have it." Torin spat each word as an accusation against Lexos. "And if I did, I'd never give it to a traitor like you."

Lexos stood back to absorb this. "It must gall you," he said, "to have me under your watchful eye all those years and to never know how long I plotted against you and those soulless dogs in Curston."

Torin wrested himself to half sitting, using his bound arms to prop him up. "You're not that clever," he said. "I never trusted you."

The truth burned in Lexos's ears, which turned nearly as red as they'd glowed when he first cast his spell.

"You know where it is." Lexos snorted at Torin.

"Yes."

A vicious smile spread across Lexos's lips. "You will tell me where it is."

Torin took a turn at smiling now. "No."

Lexos walked around Torin, giving the watcher a wide berth. He pointed at the three kids huddled near the Seal.

"If you do not tell me what I want to know, I will kill them—one by one."

Torin scowled. "You're bluffing. You don't have it in you. You're fine when it comes to ordering others to kill for you, but you don't have the steel to bloody your own hands."

"Am I so cowardly? So timid, so fearful of taking action?" Lexos sneered at Torin. "For a watcher, you're not terribly observant. If you were, you'd realize why the Key of Order failed the first time Zendric and your precious wife tried to use it."

Torin's eyes bulged in fury.

"Yes," Lexos said, satisfaction coloring his face. "I tampered with it. I made sure it would shatter."

The cleric cocked his head and leaned over toward the watcher. "I caused all those people to die." Then he glanced over at the trio in the short tunnel and whispered, "And I'll tear the life from each of those children too."

Torin closed his eyes tight. Driskoll knew his father would have covered his ears too if he'd been able to use his hands.

"You can't do this," Torin said.

"I don't think you need magic to know that I can."

Lexos stood up and walked over to the three kids huddled in the short tunnel. "So," he said slowly, "which one would you like to watch die first?"

Driskoll whimpered. Even without the effects of Lexos's spell on him, he would have been as scared as he'd ever been in his life. As it was, he couldn't shove aside enough of the fear to even think to move. There was no room left in his head to do anything but wait to die and to hope that maybe—since it would mean the end of this sheer terror—it would happen soon.

"I'm sorry!" Torin called, his voice raw with grief. Driskoll thought that Torin would have given one of his arms up right then and there if it meant he could be free.

"Kellach! Driskoll! I'm sorry! Oh, Moyra!" Torin's voice trailed off into sobs then, and Driskoll prepared himself to die.

"You'll pay for forcing my hand, Torin," Lexos said. "It didn't have to be this way."

The cleric pocketed the incomplete Key of Order, then reached out and began to chant a prayer to his cruel god. As he did, he stretched his arms out toward Kellach, and his hands began to glow with a blood red light.

Before Lexos could complete his spell, Lochinvar launched

himself from where he had wound himself around Kellach's shoulders. The dragonet let loose a high-pitched roar as he flew at Lexos, his wings and talons glinting red in the Seal's fiery light.

The cleric's words caught in his throat, and he flung up his arms to try to protect himself. Lochinvar slashed at Lexos with his tail and tore at him with his claws, shredding the cleric's robes.

For a moment, hope sprang in Driskoll's heart, shoving aside enough of the fear for him to pull his hands from his face and cheer the little clockwork creature on.

Lexos's hand snapped out and caught Lochinvar around the neck. He held the dragonet out at arm's length, ignoring the way he whipped his tail about.

"How touching," Lexos said, snarling at Lochinvar. "The boy wizard's toy comes to his defense while his father lays helpless at my feet."

He raised his arm to smash the dragonet to pieces on the cavern floor. "And how pathe—"

Lexos stopped himself, his arm still raised and the struggling dragonet still clutched in it. He stared at Lochinvar for a moment, his eyes wide and his mouth open. Then he threw back his head and began to laugh.

"I should have given you more credit," the cleric said to Torin. "You and that ancient wizard. I didn't think he had a clever bone left in him."

Torin kicked out at Lexos, but the cleric leaped out of his

reach. The watcher tried to squirm after the cleric, and Lexos rewarded him with a hard kick to the head. The cleric grinned the entire time.

Lochinvar growled in protest as Lexos turned his attention toward the dragonet. "Now," he said, "I will have what I came for."

With one swift move, Lexos tore Lochinvar's wings from his back. The tiny creature howled in misery and fell limp. The cleric tossed him to the side, and he skittered across the cavern floor until he crashed into the far wall.

Lexos held the wings up, a gleam of mad triumph in his ice-blue eyes. Then he drew out the rest of the Key of Order and matched it up with the wings.

They fit perfectly.

CHAPTER

24

Driskoll's mind reeled. Locky—Ssarine's creation, Zendric's gift to Kellach—Locky had held the last piece of the Key of Order all the time. The piece had been a part of him, built into him.

"Locky!" Kellach stood up and charged at Lexos, ready to tear the cleric apart with his bare hands.

Lexos laughed and cast another spell. Kellach froze in place, just as Driskoll had on the terrace of the Town Hall. His momentum caused him to fall over at the cleric's feet.

Lexos's spell of fear had worn off as Kellach had shown. Driskoll hadn't realized it because he was so terrified anyhow that it had become impossible to distinguish between the spell and what gripped his heart for real. Now that he'd seen his brother make one last attempt to stop the cleric, though, he knew he could do no less.

When he tried to move, however, Driskoll realized that the

spell which paralyzed Kellach had affected him too. A frustrated moan from Moyra told him that she had discovered the same thing. Even Torin had stopped moving at all.

"I'm taking no chances with you fools now," Lexos said. "I've come too far, done too many horrible things, for you to ruin this for me now."

Lexos stepped over Moyra, then reached down and turned Driskoll to face the Seal. "I understand you have aspirations of becoming a great bard someday, a spinner of epic tales." He chuckled to himself. "If so, you're going to want to see this."

The cleric strode up to the cracking Seal, and it seemed to Driskoll that the light streaming through the breaks in the metal gleamed brighter than ever, as if whatever stood on the other side hungered for its release.

Driskoll strained to move, even just to wiggle his nose, but nothing worked. All he could do was sit there and watch as Lexos fitted the Key of Order into the dragon design in the center of the Seal.

It matched perfectly.

Having failed to prevent Lexos from executing his plan, Driskoll wanted nothing more than to look away from what would happen next, to close his eyes and shut it all out. The spell denied him even that small blessing.

Lexos stepped back from the Seal, moving past Driskoll and out of sight, perhaps all the way to the tunnel's mouth. For a moment, nothing happened. The utter silence in the room only heightened the tension. Driskoll could hear nothing but his heaving breath and his pounding heart.

The edges of the Key of Order began to glow a pure and brilliant white. The glow diffused outward through the rest of the Seal, permeating every bit of the metal and working its way into the reddish cracks as well.

"No," Lexos said, horror creeping into his voice. "I followed their directions. I did as they asked."

If Driskoll could have moved his lips, his grin would have split his face in two. A moment later, though, it would have melted away like a snowball in a blacksmith's hearth.

The reddish glow began to grow, to devour the white light. When it reached the edges of the cracks it had once filled, Driskoll hoped that it would stop, but it kept spreading, taking over more and more of the white glow as it went, tainting its purity with its blasphemous crimson color.

The glow brightened bit by bit until it hurt Driskoll's eyes. Again he wished he could turn away, but he could do nothing but keep staring ahead, his eyes tearing up with the pain.

The light swallowed everything but the Key of Order itself. The Key hung there—solid and real, itself untouched—while all around it dissolved in the fiery glow.

Then the glow went out like a snuffed candle, and the Key of Order fell with a clang to the ground.

"Yes," Lexos breathed from somewhere behind Driskoll.

Driskoll tried to blink but could not. As his vision cleared from the dazzling light, the scent of brimstone reached his nose and nearly forced him to gag. When the spots faded from his eyes, he could see through the gate behind the sundered Seal, straight into the Abyss.

In the realm beyond, the gate stood on a high tower that looked out over a turbulent vista of chaos and pain. Pillars of magma belched from a lava-filled lake, vaporizing some of the horned and winged creatures that filled the sky. Blood-red thunderheads cracked with blackish lightning, the peals of which sounded like the wailing of a million damned souls. In the plains below, countless creatures clashed in an unending battle.

A bat-winged demon flew in through the gate then, skimming right over the top of Driskoll's head. It landed next to Lexos and let loose an evil laugh that made Driskoll wish he'd been deaf from birth.

The demon spoke in a tongue that Driskoll could not understand. The noises of the words made him wish to clean out his ears with a corkscrew. Lexos laughed along with the demon, in horrible, disgusting glee.

Another demon flew in through the gate where the Seal had once stood. Then another and countless others, until Driskoll imagined they stacked the cavern behind him to the ceiling.

After them came dozens of other demons of all different kinds. Some looked like the quasit he'd seen that morning, which now seemed so long ago. Others resembled Nahemah, the succubus that had impersonated his mother a few months ago.

A host of man-sized demons marched by, their tiny wings flapping on their backs and their snakelike tails wiggling behind them as they went. They carried tridents, swords, and bows, each with jagged edges that looked like they would slice open the hands of any who tried to grab them, yet these scaly-skinned soldiers handled them with ease. They stank of brimstone, and Driskoll could feel the awful heat of the Abyss radiating from them as they passed him by.

A pack of three-headed dogs with crimson skin like that of a lizard charged past next. Where their greenish spittle fell, it burned, pitting even the rocky floor. They lunged forward in groups of six, each leashed by red-hot chains to the front of a three-wheeled chariot that raced behind them on spiked rims.

As the creatures moved past Driskoll on their way into the chamber behind him, he realized that the long stream never paused; instead, it pushed through to the rest of the Dungeons of Doom beyond. From there, he knew, they would work their way to the surface. Once out in the open air, he could only guess where they might go, but his heart told him that they would descend on hapless Curston all too soon.

At one point, the spell holding Driskoll frozen wore off, but he couldn't bring himself to move. Something told him that the moment he tried to turn, run, or even scream, any demon within a claw's reach of him would shred him into tiny, wet pieces. Or maybe just throw him through the gate to let him live out his last moments in the absolute terror of the Abyss.

When the last of the chariots filed past, Driskoll still held his position. His muscles ached, and he felt like he might fall over at any moment, but he couldn't bring himself to turn around to see if the demons had all gone just yet.

That's when he heard Lexos chuckling again.

"Ah," the cleric said. "Alone again at last. Now that you've seen the army of demons set to descend upon that worthless town of ours and strip it from the face of the earth, my fun is over."

Driskoll fell over onto his back with a whimper. He forced his cramped muscles to work just enough so that he could turn to see Lexos grinning at him, Moyra, Kellach, and Torin.

Moyra knelt right where she had before, her back to Driskoll now, but he could see in the slump of her shoulders that she was already beaten. He imagined she'd find the same look on his face if she were to glance backward. Driskoll could not conceive how Curston could stand against such a tremendous force of evil as had just marched past him on its way to war.

Kellach started to chant something again, but Lexos stepped over and kicked him in the chest, cutting off his spell.

"Valiant to the end?" Lexos said. "Perhaps you and the others were worthy of being named Knights of the Silver Dragon. Pity you shall meet the same terrible end as those who went before you."

Torin cursed at the cleric, using language that would have shocked Driskoll just an hour before. After witnessing that procession of demons, though, he wondered if anything could ever shock him again.

Then Lexos began to chant a horrible prayer filled with even worse blasphemies. Driskoll knew that this had to be the end. The cleric would slaughter them all with his death magic and offer their fresh souls up as an offering to his vicious god.

Arcs of black-red power crackled along Lexos's arms and hands, dancing through his fingers.

"Good-bye," Lexos said.

The cleric opened his lips to say something else, but before he could even start, a bolt of lightning streaked out from behind Driskoll and lanced Lexos straight through.

Lexos stared past Driskoll in gape-mouthed horror.

Driskoll spun around.

At that moment, he would not have been surprised to see St. Cuthbert himself stroll through the gate and strike Lexos down with his cudgel.

Instead, he watched as Zendric strode through the gate, a smoking wand held before him.

To be continued . . .

Don't miss the exciting conclusion
to the Revelations Duet

THE DRAGONS REVEALED

As fiends soar the skies and monsters prowl the streets,
the Knights have but one hope left: the dragons that
long ago pledged to protect their order. Zendric readies
the ritual for recalling their winged allies, while the
Knights race back to the Dungeons to restore the seal.
There's just one thing they aren't prepared for: a traitor
in their midst.

Return to where it all began!

Secret of the Spiritkeeper

Knights of the Silver Dragon, Book 1
By Matt Forbeck

Zendric the wizard has been robbed and enchanted into a lifeless sleep. His spiritkeeper is missing, and only Moyra, Kellach, and Driskoll know how to find it. Deep in the Dungeons of Doom, they must outsmart a zombie, goblins, even an owlbear. But can the Knights unlock the secret of the spiritkeeper in time to save their friend?

CHAPTER 1

"Curse it, boy!" Zendric said. "Put that thing down!"

Kellach nearly dropped the small, transparent ball in his hand. Tall and thin, he looked like a fourteen-year-old scarecrow dressed in stained apprentice's robes. The know-it-all look he normally wore on his face vanished.

Zendric stalked over and snatched the shiny globe from Kellach's hands.

"Fool!" the wizard said. "You have no idea the danger you're toying with!"

Driskoll, Kellach's twelve-year-old brother, cowered by the doorway. He had arrived moments ago to walk Kellach home from his lesson. Now he wished he had been a little late.

Zendric hoisted the globe up to the light streaming in through one of the tower's many windows. The globe seemed filled with murky smoke, and its golden bands glinted in the sunshine.

"If you never teach me anything, then how am I to know better?" Kellach said. He stepped up to the wizard's face, nose to nose with the old elf. "I've studied with you for two years, and I barely know how to light a fire!"

The wizard snorted and turned away. He carefully set the globe back into its place on the mantle. "I've told you this globe is off-limits. If you would spend as much effort on your lessons as you do on irritating me—"

Zendric bit his tongue. He turned back to face Kellach.

"Kellach, you are the most promising student I've ever had. But if you can't learn to respect such things of power, how can you be trusted with difficult spells? If Jourdain—"

"You leave my mother out of this!" Kellach poked Zendric in the chest.

Zendric stopped cold. He looked down at Kellach's finger, the tip of which still pushed against the wizard's robes. When his head came back up, his eyes were filled with wrath.

"You ungrateful whelp!" Zendric said. "I don't care how good a friend Jourdain was. You are *never* to cross my threshold again!"

"But you're my teacher," said Kellach.

"Not any more!"

Zendric chanted something quick and angry. Energy crackled through the air. Driskoll could feel the hairs on the back of his neck stand on end. Kellach backed away, stuttering an apology, but it was too late.

An invisible force lashed out and punched Kellach flat in the chest, driving him straight out the door.

Zendric growled in frustration, turned around, and headed straight for Driskoll. The boy froze for a moment, then tried to scramble under a desk. Zendric grabbed him by the collar and hauled him to his feet.

The wizard glared down at Driskoll. He shoved Kellach's pack into Driskoll's arms.

"Do your brother a favor, lad. Keep him away from here. The next time I won't be so kind."

With that, Driskoll found himself out on the street. He turned around to protest on his brother's behalf, but before he could utter a word the thick, ironbound door slammed in his face. He heard the lock fall into place.

Driskoll looked back around to see Kellach sitting on the cobblestone street, gaping at the wizard's tower. Driskoll shook his head. He walked up to his brother and handed him his pack.

"You've really made a mess of it this time," Driskoll said.

"Shut up." Kellach stood up, shouldered his pack, and started walking west. Driskoll followed close on his heels.

"Wait until Dad hears about this," Driskoll said.

Kellach didn't turn around. "You're not going to tell him."

It was all Driskoll could do to keep up with his brother until they reached Main Square. During the peak of the day, Main Square was the busiest place in all of Curston. Dozens of merchants kept tents and booths here, selling their merchandise to anyone in need or want of their wares. Now, though, the place stood nearly empty, with the exception of a few rows of booths kept by the richest merchants. Only two remained, haggling with a group of stragglers before shutting down business for the night.

Just beyond the booths, at the center of Main Square, stood a white marble obelisk, the most recognizable landmark in town. The obelisk rose thirty feet into the air, straight out of the center of a massive design in the square's pavement. The design allowed the obelisk to function as part of a humongous sundial.

The surrounding buildings cast long shadows over the square. The Cathedral of St. Cuthbert of the Cudgel soared above them all, its bell tower stabbing even higher than the top of Zendric's distant home. Atop the bell tower's peak, the circled cross of St. Cuthbert looked down over the square, like the eye of the demigod himself, searching for any incursion of evil.

The sun's rays caught the large rubies in St. Cuthbert's cross and set them ablaze. Driskoll glanced at the sundial. It would be less than an hour before all of Curston lay blanketed in darkness.

"Come on, Kellach," Driskoll said. "We'd better go home."

"I'm not going home." Kellach set his jaw.

"What are you going to do, join a group of fortune hunters and head for the ruins?" Driskoll laughed.

Kellach had often mentioned such plans, but only in jest. Centuries old, the ruins lay a few miles outside of Curston. Once the most prosperous city in the region, the ruins now lay deserted, with the exception of the occasional group of treasure hunters. Five years ago, one such group had broken a seal deep in the dungeons beneath the ruins, releasing hordes of demons and things viler still. The incident had nearly destroyed neighboring Curston. Even five years later, everyone had to be on guard against evil beasts from the ruins wreaking havoc on the town.

"The ruins," Kellach muttered. "That's not a bad idea."

"You're cracked," Driskoll said. "It's nearly curfew already. No one stays outside after dark."

"That's a legend they tell to scare *children*." Kellach looked at his brother pointedly as he emphasized that last word. "People walk the streets of Curston at all hours. Dad spends the night out here all the time."

"He's the captain of the watch," Driskoll said. "That's his job. Besides, he's surrounded by other watchers."

Kellach didn't seem to hear him. "Forget about fortune hunting," he said to himself. "I can be a modern Knight of the Silver Dragon instead."

"What are you babbling about?"

Kellach snapped his attention back to Driskoll. "Zendric used to talk about the Knights of the Silver Dragon all the time. He was one of them. They were founded back when Curston was still called Promise, in the town's early days."

Driskoll rolled his eyes. "Thanks for the history lesson."

Kellach ignored him. "The wealthy merchants of the town formed the Knights as a group of honorable warriors. Their job was to protect the city from outside threats."

"If they were so amazing, where are they now?"

Kellach shrugged. "Over the years, they slowly faded away. The last of them disappeared just after the Sundering of the Seal."

"So you want to model your career after a bunch of people who went missing?"

"Why not? If they were still around now, they'd be begging me to join them. You heard Zendric call me his best student ever. Plus, there's not a part of Curston I'm afraid to walk through. I know this town like the back of my—*oompf*!"

Someone ran headlong into the boys, knocking them both to the ground. They were a tangle of arms, legs, and heads. Driskoll's eyes landed on the person's face, and he recognized her instantly.

"Moyra!" he blurted as he pulled himself free. The girl— who was barely a year older than Driskoll—wore simple but well-used clothes, chosen to be the same gray color as the stones used in most of Curston's buildings. The idea was to help her blend in. But more often than not, it failed miserably, due not so much to the clothes as to the person wearing them.

Moyra's face was flushed, and she was breathing hard. She rolled off of Kellach and landed nimbly on her feet. As she did, she let loose a string of curses that would have made Zendric blush. "And thanks to you, I'm dead!" she finished.

As Kellach and Driskoll got to their feet, Moyra finally saw their faces, and she lit up like a lamp. "Boys! It's you! Thank the gods!" She threw her long arms around the brothers.

As Moyra pulled back from the embrace, a herd of footsteps came thundering toward them.

"From the sound of things," she said, calmer now, "it seems I could use your help."

ACKNOWLEDGMENTS

Special thanks to
Nina Hess, Emily Fiegenschuh, and Peter Archer.

Written by series creator Matt Forbeck, this special two-part KNIGHTS
OF THE SILVER DRAGON adventure will rock Curston to the core!

REVELATIONS

Five years ago, treasure hunters destroyed a seal deep in the Dungeons
of Doom, releasing hordes of monsters upon the people of Curston.
An ancient prophecy predicted the city would face the fiends
from the Abyss again.

PROPHECY OF THE DRAGONS
REVELATIONS, PART 1

It's up to Moyra, Driskoll and Kellach to make sure the prophecy doesn't
come true. It won't be easy with the return of Lexos, who seeks a key that
has kept the seal locked for the last five years. Lexos has a few surprises up
his sleeve, but what the Knights find behind the seal might be
the biggest surprise of them all.

THE DRAGONS REVEALED
REVELATIONS, PART 2

As fiends soar the skies and monsters prowl the streets, the Knights have
but one hope left: the dragons that long ago pledged to protect their order.
Zendric readies the ritual for recalling their winged allies, while the
Knights race back to the Dungeons to restore the seal. There is just one
thing they aren't prepared for: a traitor in their midst.

Ask for KNIGHTS OF THE SILVER DRAGON books
at your favorite bookstore!

For more information visit www.knightsofthesilverdragon.com

www.mirrorstonebooks.com

MORE ADVENTURES
FOR THE

MYSTERY OF THE WIZARD'S TOMB

Are the Knights prepared for what they'll find inside the wizard's tomb?

February 2006

MARK OF THE YUAN-TI

Is Driskoll's new pet really harmless? Or is there more to his snake than meets the eye?

April 2006

REALM OF THE RAKSHASAS

Can the Knights free Moyra and the rest of the kidnapped children from the rakshasas' evil spell before it's too late?

October 2006

ROOM OF THE EYES

Can the Knights unravel the riddle of the Room of the Eyes before Kellach goes to jail?

December 2006

**Ask for KNIGHTS OF THE SILVER DRAGON books
at your favorite bookstore!**

For more information visit www.knightsofthesilverdragon.com

www.mirrorstonebooks.com

THE NEW ADVENTURES

A Practical Guide to Dragons
By Sindri Suncatcher

Sindri Suncatcher—wizard's apprentice—opens up
his personal notebooks to share his knowledge of these
awe-inspiring creatures, from the life cycle of a kind copper
dragon to the best way to counteract a red dragon's fiery
breath. This lavishly illustrated guide showcases the wide
array of fantastic dragons encountered on the world of Krynn.

The perfect companion to the Dragonlance: The New
Adventures series, for both loyal fans and new readers alike.

Sindri Suncatcher is a three-and-a-half foot tall kender,
who enjoys storytelling, collecting magical tokens, and
fighting dragons. He lives in Solamnia and is currently
studying magic under the auspices of the black-robed
wizard Maddoc. You can catch Sindri in the midst of
his latest adventure in *The Wayward Wizard*.

For more information visit www.mirrorstonebooks.com

For ages ten and up.

THE NEW ADVENTURES

THE ELIDOR TRILOGY
Ree Soesbee

CROWN OF THIEVES

As Elidor struggles to keep the crown out of the hands of
an evil wizard, he finds himself drawn back to the one place
that frightens him the most: his own past.
November 2005

THE CRYSTAL CHALICE

As the Defiler's curse holds Vael's health hostage, Elidor searches for
a way to rescue her without succumbing to the evil wizard's demands.
March 2006

CITY OF FORTUNE

Vael lies frozen between life and death, and Elidor must save her.
The answer lies in a chalice that holds a powerful wish. But danger
awaits those with wishes, for the Defiler still lurks in the shadows.
July 2006

**Ask for DRAGONLANCE: THE NEW ADVENTURES
books at your favorite bookstore!**

For more information visit www.mirrorstonebooks.com

For ages ten and up.

THE NEW ADVENTURES

THE TRINISTYR TRILOGY

The Trinistyr
Ancient holy relic
Cursed symbol of power
Key to Nearra's future . . . or her destruction

WIZARD'S CURSE

Christina Woods

Imbued with vestiges of Asvoria's power, Nearra is convinced
she can restore her magical heritage. Will Nearra find
the strength to break the wizard's curse?
September 2005

WIZARD'S BETRAYAL

Jeff Sampson

Betrayals come to light. New powers arise. And a startling
revelation threatens to destroy Nearra, once and for all.
January 2006

WIZARD'S RETURN

Dan Willis

Can the companions stand together and fight the final battle
for Nearra and Jirah's future?
May 2006

**Ask for Dragonlance: The New Adventures
books at your favorite bookstore!**

For more information visit www.mirrorstonebooks.com

For ages ten and up.